A LORD OF HER OWN

CHRISTINA MCKNIGHT

LA LOMA ELITE PUBLISHING

COPYRIGHT

A LORD OF HER OWN

Marcus Adair, the Duke of Beargarner, has a secret: due to the gross overspending of his father, his dukedom is on the verge of bankruptcy. When his friend suggests he court Lady Godiva, daughter of the Earl of Garland, it seems like a marriage of convenience is the perfect solution. She'll get the benefits of his title and protection, and he'll get access to her father's shipping empire. But when Marcus meets Godiva, he's enchanted by her beauty and her bravery. A marriage in name only is no longer an option.

Yet Godiva has been burned before, and she's vowed not to trust any man. Shunned by the ton for her portly appearance, Godiva has already had three marriage proposals broken. All that remains in her future, she thinks, is loneliness. Marcus seems like he could offer her more, a life that truly has joy in it, until she learns he's seeking her out for her father's contacts. With this new betrayal, Godiva is certain she's done with love.

To win her heart, Marcus must convince Godiva that she's truly the bold, brilliant woman he sees. Can Godiva forget the past to welcome a future with her lord?

DEDICATION

For my friend.
This book would not have happened without your superior
guidance and wisdom!

CHAPTER 1

"*D*o stop flailing about, Mother." Lady Godiva's sturdy frame was no match for her mother's constant dramatics as they made their way above stairs and to her chambers. "One would not think a fainting spell would cause such convolutions. Are you certain I need not send for a physician?"

She should have accepted the footman's offer of assistance before her mother had motioned the man away, for surely Godiva would acquire several bruises for her kindness.

It'd taken all of her strength to haul Lady Garland up the servant's back staircase to avoid the prying eyes of the *ton*. And it was overly convenient her father had mysteriously disappeared moments before her mother's latest episode commenced.

"No, my dear," Lady Garland—Beatrice—moaned. "I shall be quite the thing after a few moment's rest."

Godiva doubted if her mother had ever been considered "quite the thing," but she knew better than to speculate this out loud. If she dared, it was likely her mother would embark on another long-winded fable about the glory of her youth; how she'd been courted by no less than three men before settling on Godiva's father, a mere earl.

Not that Godiva saw this as an unattainable feat...she'd been courted by three men as well.

And unceremoniously jilted, in turn, by each.

But that reminder would send Lady Garland into another dizzy spell. Her daughter's unsuccessful, ill-fated courtships were never spoken of—not in public and especially not in private.

Therefore, Godiva kept her sense of failure to herself, squared her shoulders, and continued to yank the woman down the last hall and safely into her dimly lit chamber, the crackle and pop of the fire breaking the quiet as its recently stoked flames cast the room in ever-moving shadows.

As soon as the door closed, her mother pulled away from Godiva's grasp and smoothed her evening gown. "I do say that was a fine show, a marvelous show, if I do say so myself."

"What?" It was the height of embarrassment if Godiva were to speak on the matter.

"Oh, dear heavens, my girl." The exasperation in her mother's words likely mirrored the look on Godiva's face. "The nerve of Lord Haston, thinking he could garner a place on your dance card. Does he not know all of society is aware of his quirks?"

Godiva was taken aback by the proclamation. "You mean to say, you fainted dead away—in front of a crowded ball-room, no less—to extricate me from my next dance partner?" Her mother's cunning behavior never ceased to amaze and confound her. And the *ton* was far more aware of Lady Garland's quirks.

Her mother's sly smirk confirmed everything.

Even in the dimness and shifting shadows of the room, Godiva saw the familiar spark light her mother's eyes.

Godiva's head ached. "Bloody hell!"

"Do not curse," Beatrice scolded. "It is very unladylike, and...dare I say, befitting a mere baroness? Do aim higher, lass." Her mother tended to fall back on her Scottish roots when excitement and mischief got the best of her. Although, as far as Godiva knew, her mother never had so much as seen the Scottish border and rarely traveled outside their London townhouse.

"You cannot keep doing these things merely because you are dismayed about something as trivial as my choice of a dance partner."

"I most certainly can and will." Lady Garland sat in her favorite chair, an overstuffed monstrosity, complete with hanging tassels and gilded, engraved legs. The puce fabric matched the countess's dress impeccably. "Do be a dear and fetch my fan." She waved her hand in front of her face. "It is dreadfully stuffy in here."

Godiva took in the chaos that was her mother's private chamber—in such disarray she could reasonably believe a small child had made it so during a particularly colossal tantrum. Not a thing was in its rightful place. Her brushes sat upon a small stool before the hearth. Her privacy screen perched so close to the exit that it would likely fall over if one pushed the door too wide. A large stack of feather-stuffed pillows was mounted by her dressing closet, forming a fort of sorts.

She hadn't any notion of where to begin her search. If she were made to climb into her mother's makeshift encamp-ment, it would likely collapse about her, smothering her in pillows the size of small horse carts.

Luckily, her mother took pity on her only daughter, lifting her hand and pointing to the screen positioned close to the door.

Godiva eyed her mother's privacy screen, realizing she'd

rather risk collapsing the pillow fort than see what lay beyond the partition.

The sooner she retrieved the bloody fan, the sooner she could escape the room and return to the ball below.

How hard could it be to find a measly fan? Godiva had nearly a dozen in her chamber, although they were arranged neatly in a rainbow color pattern on her dressing table—easily located.

Slipping behind the screen, Godiva realized her mistake and regretted catching her mother when she fainted. She should have let her fall to the floor...maybe it would have knocked some sense into her addled brain.

"It looks marvelous, does it not?" her mother's singsong voice called from her place beyond the partition. "I debated all morning on the perfect spot for her. I do think she'll enjoy the view."

Godiva was convinced—Lady Garland had officially gone mad.

Stark raving mad. Godiva only prayed the malady was not one commonly inherited.

"Thankfully, she is long expired and must care less about her current scenic view."

And Godiva did not doubt her mother had given the woman a rather extensive view. The painting of Lady Godiva, Countess of Mercia, her namesake and supposed great-aunt several times removed, was much like everything else in her mother's chamber, overly gilded and out of place. Yet, strangely befitting Beatrice.

"You are much like her, my child," Beatrice confided. "Though I sense you fight it at every turn."

Godiva tilted her head and squinted her eyes at the painting...next, she hummed a bit.

Still, she did not see the resemblance between herself and the woman portrayed before her.

4

Firstly, Godiva was baffled at how the portly lady had attained such a reclining position, her bosom exposed to the artist, without falling head-first off the settee she was draped across. It defied all she'd read about the forces of nature. History held that Lady Godiva had this particular painting commissioned after she'd flouted her husband's edict and ridden the streets of their small town, stripped bare, to earn her cruel husband's respect and notice. Their people suffered while her husband lived as if all on their land thrived.

If she were truthful, Godiva doubted the woman was in any way a relation to her or her mother's family. The portrait was more likely found in a dusty attic decades before, brushed off, and hung up on the wall to elevate her family's sense of import, resulting in a suitably compelling story of maternal association that developed over the years.

Even more unfortunate was the fact that Godiva had been born a plump baby, rounded to excess—and had stayed much the same throughout her childhood and into adulthood. However, her mother had long held there were worse things than to be named after a countess of famed beauty and bold-ness of nature.

Godiva was not so convinced.

"Do you see it, Godiva?" her mother called.

She closed her eyes briefly to dispel the image of her namesake's ample breasts partially spilling from the top of her gown as she reclined over the lounge.

Another unfortunate certainty: the depiction was appar-ently seared into her mind—for eternity.

If only she could convince her mother to leave the dreadful painting in one place. It would make it all the easier for Godiva to avoid stumbling upon the sight, but her luck never held. Last week it had hung above their supper table, resulting in her and her father passing on several meals. Just this morning, it was suspended in the grand foyer where every new visitor would garner a glance of the woman's wares. Thankfully, her father had put his foot down solidly—which did not often happen—and demanded the portrait be moved until after the evening's party. Her mother had agreed, not wishing the spotlight to be removed from her daughter.

Godiva hardly believed the lady would have commissioned such a piece had she known her bosom would one day be on display for every English gentleperson unfortunate enough to cross her family's threshold.

Scanning the small area again, Godiva didn't see the gem-encrusted fan anywhere. "No, Mother, it is not here. Are you positive you did not leave it below?"

Quiet greeted her from beyond the screen. She peeked around to see why her mother, for possibly the first time in her existence, remained silent.

"Mother!" she called. "Do listen. I have no intention of spending my entire evening here with you."

"I was only listening to the music below." Beatrice stood quickly, her fan slipping from the folds of her dress, landing on the rug-covered floor without a sound.

Both eyed the discarded fan as the light from the hearth moved to spotlight the delicate accessory.

"You are incorrigible!" Godiva proclaimed, only barely managing not to stomp her foot. "I must be going. Time may yet allow a short dance for Lord Haston and me." And she hoped she could return to the ballroom before the song ended. Haston was a kind, if not overly captivating, man. He listened intently when she spoke and offered her refreshments when appropriate. He never sought to lead her into any scandalous incidents.

Which was much more than she could say for her earlier beaus.

Reprobates and scoundrels, the lot of them. Sometimes it

was hard for her to pinpoint one awful trait worse than the rest. Their only redeeming quality—if one could call it that— was that their titles and fortunes were beyond reproach.

But one does not learn manners or loyalty or gain integrity from a title alone.

Godiva had learned that the hard way—on multiple occasions.

Her cheeks heated at her gullible follies of the past.

Beatrice huffed. "Do tell me you are not standing there daydreaming of *Haston*."

Her mother's words pushed the thoughts of her ill-fated past back where they belonged—buried deep, right where she wished she could put the bodies of Lords Danderfur, Plumberly, and Canterbourne. Alas, all three men thrived... and continued to move amongst the highest in London society.

It was only Godiva who lived with the aftermath of the scandals.

Lord Canterbourne had recovered so completely from the ordeal he was now betrothed to another lucky lady. Godiva truly hoped her dearest friend, Delilah, experienced an altogether different marquis than Godiva had faced the previous season.

"Now that you have located your misplaced fan, I think I will be on my way." There was no need to confess she hadn't been daydreaming about Haston, but instead reliving a nightmare of far greater proportion. "I will tell Father you are resting for a spell and will return shortly."

The perturbed look left her mother's face, and she smiled. "My dear, wonderful daughter. Not a day passes I do not thank whatever divine being gave you to me." Flipping her fan open, she quickly moved it back and forth in front of her face. The slight breeze from the hurried effort pushed her long curls over her shoulder.

"If you would consider pinning your hair atop your head, you would stay much cooler and not succumb to overheating so much." It was the argument mother and daughter embarked on at least a dozen times each season.

"You know I cannot pull my hair up, for it would make me appear the old woman. I might as well don a hideous cap with plumes and feathers aplenty." Beatrice's free hand swept her bouncing curls forward. "And what will happen to me then if I admit my age? You know as well as I, dear, not a soul in London would believe I am any older than you."

Godiva self-consciously patted her upswept hair, nestled securely at her crown in the severe style she preferred over her mother's flowing flair. If her mother fought the passage of time, then it was Godiva who embraced it, wallowed in it, and prayed society would leave her to it.

"Good eve, Mother." She wouldn't be seeing her again this evening. Her mother's aversion to society was not altogether new, and Godiva was certain she'd busy herself here until her father retired at the end of the night. "I hope you are feeling better on the morrow."

CHAPTER 2

*M*arcus Adair, the sixth Duke of Beargarner, paced the hall, his feet likely wearing the threaded rug beneath him thin as the confines of the corridor shrank around him, making it difficult to draw significant breath. His lungs burned, and the soles of his feet ached from his determined movement. He pivoted sharply and strode back down the seemingly never-ending hall for the tenth time—his wide shoulders and long stride dwarfing the walkway as his patience waned.

Where was the confounded woman?

He'd kept a close eye on Lady Godiva all evening, attempting to gain an introduction on several occasions, though his efforts fell short repeatedly, only adding to his current frustration. She was one of the most elusive creatures he'd had the misfortune of trailing. She'd danced nearly every set, conversed with every person present save for himself, and had—if it were even possible—disappeared from the room without a trace.

And he hadn't caught sight of her since.

That must have been nearly half an hour ago—and the evening was quickly drawing to an end.

If he were a paranoid fellow, Marcus might wonder if she knew he sought her, and it was *she* who avoided *him*.

The lady was not at all what Marcus had expected. She wasn't the pitiful, dejected spinster clamoring for a marriage proposal as Canterbourne had insinuated. Nothing about the woman bespoke desperation. In fact, her every action pointed to her poise and grace—an inner confidence that shone brightly.

Bloody hell if he didn't find the woman elegance personified.

He ran his finger through his hair, dispelling the maudlin musing. There wasn't time, nor did he have the energy, to fall prey to such thinking.

The night was waning, and he'd been unsuccessful in gaining her notice. He could not keep up appearances in London for long, nor live off Canterbourne's generosity forever, all while hiding from those who searched for him.

The only place Lady Godiva could have disappeared to was a room above stairs. This being her family home, it was more than likely she'd sought a reprieve from the crowd in her private chamber.

He wouldn't dwell on the possibility she favored another and had slipped away for a private word. Although, he had watched her dance with many of London's most sought after men. At her advanced age, the *ton* would likely ignore it if she did seek out such engagements. He did not agree with that particular sentiment of society but understood these were not ideals he was likely to change or influence.

"Your Grace?" The nasally, feminine voice came from the direction of the stairs, which led to the ballroom below. Marcus could not fathom how he had ever found her voice attractive. "I had wondered where you'd run off to."

Her hand landed on his shoulder and gently kneaded the tension that laced through his neck and back.

The gentleness of her touch didn't last long as her fingers stiffened to press more securely into his shoulder, and she whispered, "I would loathe thinking you are avoiding me, Marcus." The threat wasn't even thinly veiled.

She knew the power she wheeled—and she expertly used it to her advantage.

"Gwendolyn." He didn't turn to face her. "What can I do for you?" His clipped, cold words should have been enough to have her spinning on her heels and fleeing for safety, but they were no match for her colder heart and callous ways.

When she didn't issue a demand or screech in anger, he relented and turned toward her.

She was everything a woman of the *ton* was expected to be: willowy with emerald eyes, sun-kissed golden hair, and a porcelain-pale complexion. If he didn't know the darkness hidden so skillfully in her eyes, she'd appear a beautiful, fragile doll.

Gwendolyn was everything he'd come to despise in the fairer sex. She might look as sweet as a kitten to the unknowing observer, but her gaze was keen and her memory long.

"I expected a dance."

"You expect much from a man who owes you naught." Marcus *owed* her even less than nothing if that were possible. He'd tried to give her everything, but she had determined him worthless and unsuitable when his creditors had come calling.

Laughing, she slid her hand from his shoulder and down his pressed shirt to rest at the front of his trousers. His body knew her wicked ways too, not responding to the touch that used to send him into a frenzy of need.

"Come now, Marcus," she purred deep in her throat—

another sound that would have caused him physical pain from want not long ago. "I know too much for you to ignore me. Now, let us return to the ballroom and dance for all to watch."

He needed to be rid of Gwen, if not from his life entirely, then from at least this one hallway. Stepping back, he said, "Gwen, I have a matter of import to discuss with Lord Garland. Afterwards, you shall have our dance." At her skeptical look, he continued, "No, make that two. Two dances."

When she smiled, letting out a burst of calculated laughter, Marcus knew he'd convinced her.

"I do not understand why you insist on having me chase you, Marcus, when we both know you always give me what I want."

The truth was, he could never be enough, possess enough, to make her content—nor did he have any urge to travel down that treacherous path again.

"Hurry back to the ballroom." He forced an uneasy smile. "I will follow as soon as I've concluded with our host."

"Do not keep me waiting, Your Grace," she said. In the past, she'd addressed him formally in hopes of convincing him that she'd make a suitable duchess. But he'd quickly learned not a moment of peace would come his way as long as she was linked to him. "I have missed you so, my dearest Marcus."

No doubt she had missed him...the gifts and attention he'd lavished on her when she'd thought his coin limitless. It was possible she demanded his attention to make another lord jealous.

With one final scorching glance, she turned and sauntered back down the hall, her finely covered backside swaying in a way that used to drive his younger self to distraction. How he'd ever been so naïve was still a wonder to him. He saw her for who she actually was now: a conniving, indifferent woman who preyed on the insecurities of others. One who took what she wanted, leaving only destruction in her wake.

His responsibility to his estate and his people—after his father left them all destitute from his excessive ways—came before all else. Marcus now understood the significance of every pound. The extravagant cost of repairs to his estate was highly preferable to the excessive cost of one ball gown or strand of pearls sent to an ungrateful lover. Though it was not Gwen's fault he was in the position he was in—that fault fell on both his father and Marcus himself. They both had their proclivities. His father had been fond of gambling and unsecured business ventures, while Marcus's eye had strayed to a pretty face and flattering, curvy backside.

As Gwen rounded the corner and disappeared, a weight collided with him from behind, nearly causing him to fall to the floor. His arm shot out to steady himself against the wall before turning.

"Oh, your legs are as thick as tree trunks, exquisite..." a woman stuttered, stepping back. He watched as her eyes travelled the length of him—although, it was more her bouncing off him as a result of their collision. "My apologies if I have injured you in any way."

He'd been so distracted by Gwen that Marcus hadn't heard the woman approaching. "Oh, no, I am unscathed by your onslaught." Marcus immediately wanted to turn tail and run—both because he'd compared their impact to an onslaught, and because he'd been caught lurking in a darkened hall of a home that was decidedly not his. "Did you refer to me as a tree?"

"Only if you compared my faux pas to an onslaught." Her brow rose in question, and her eyes sparkled in the pale glow of the wall sconces, highlighting the upsweep of her thick, dark hair.

He inclined his head slightly in deference. "I wouldn't dare, Lady Godiva."

Her face clouded with confusion for only a moment, and Marcus dreaded having to admit he'd been hoping to gain her notice for a better part of the evening. Thankfully, she gave him a tentative smile before continuing, "I do beg your pardon, but these are the private rooms of Lord and Lady Garland." Her voice was soft, almost a familiar melody, and far preferable to that of the woman who'd just returned to the ballroom. "If you do not mind—"

"It *is* Lady Godiva, correct?" He couldn't believe his good fortune. "I do beg your pardon…" It was most assuredly not a wise idea to tell her he'd been wandering the halls in search of her.

"Do we know one another?" she asked, her expression narrowed, assessing him.

"Not formally, I fear." Marcus took a step back, bowing deeply. "I am the Duke of Beargarner."

"My." Her hand came to rest just above the neckline of her gown. "Bear…your name certainly suits your dark looks and overly long hair."

"Beargarner," he corrected. "And if my hair offends you, I shall have it cut with all haste."

"I said nothing of the sort, only that society deems shorter locks to be more *civilized*." She patted her own dark hair, her hand searching for any tendrils that might have sprung loose when they'd bumped into one another. "My apologies. I cannot seem to keep words inside this evening."

Marcus took a moment to look her up and down as she'd done unto him previously. She was as pleasingly shapely up close, her hair swept up, allowing him a view of her elegant neck and a slight dimple in her cheek when she smiled. How had her natural beauty escaped his notice all evening?

It was almost inconceivable this woman before him had

ever been dubbed portly and homely. No woman with an ounce of Lady Godiva's wit could be considered ordinary.

"Your Grace?"

He wracked his brain for a charming reply, anything that could muster a semblance of *his* wit. "Do forgive my dreadful manners. I sought an introduction earlier—"

"To whom?"

"Why, you, of course, my lady." He paused, but when she only stared, he continued, "As I was saying, I sought an introduction earlier. I had hoped to add my name to your dance card."

She looked down at the card hanging loosely from her wrist and then back to him. "Why ever would you seek to dance with me?"

Marcus was uncertain about how to answer her question. He was a duke and unattached; no lady turned down his request for a dance nor questioned his interest. Telling her the truth was certainly out of the question. As was elaborating on her beauty, since she didn't appear the sort to buy into flattery. He'd expected to walk into the ballroom, sweep her into his arms for the first dance, and be discussing her dowry with her father by morning.

"Are you hard of hearing?" Her eyes widened, and her voice rose. She looked beyond him toward the staircase. "Is there someone I can fetch to help you?"

It finally struck him—she thought him daft.

"Can I accompany you back to the ballroom, Lady Godiva?"

"I do not know, can you?"

He was unsure who was more frustrated at their absurd exchange, though he had enough sense to know she was finding great amusement at his expense.

Maybe it would be safer to take his chances with Gwen. Marrying her would not give him access to a fleet of cargo ships, but she had the money to buy Marcus out of debtor's prison. If that weight were lifted, he could focus on the matter of his future and restoring his family's honor—but then he would be tied to Gwen for all eternity, and that would make his family legacy worthless. She had no interest in a family, either existing or one to come. That point, she'd been very clear about since he'd made her acquaintance.

Squaring his shoulders, he tried again. "My lady, I would be honored to escort you to your father."

"Ah-ha," she said, placing her hand in the same spot Gwen's had sat, yet Lady Godiva's touch was warm where Gwen's had been frigid. "One should never ask permission for something they desire, but demand what they want."

"I will remember such in the future, my lady." She was clearly not the shy and reserved spinster he'd set his sights on wooing. Under closer inspection, she was quite young and her body, while rounded a bit more than was the thing in society, was perfectly proportioned. Dare he say voluptuous? "After our return, you will accept my offer for our first dance."

"And why ever would I do that?" Her hand sat weightlessly on his arm as they descended the stairs to the main floor and the chords of a cotillion in mid-song floated up to greet them. "My sets are spoken for for the remainder of the evening."

"Surely you can find a free spot for my name." He wondered why she seemed so averse to adding his name to her list. "Who is promised your next dance?" Marcus took hold of her card as they reached the hall leading to the ballroom. He was being overly forward, however he had but a few brief moments to convince her. "The Earl of Plumberly —I can see why you are leery of calling off your dance with him."

He feigned shock, raising his brow.

"And you think yourself worthier of a dance than the earl?" Surprising him further, she mirrored his stunned expression. "The earl and I have had a long friendship. I do not think he will take kindly to being jilted."

Marcus wanted to laugh at her choice of words. While he hadn't spent much time in London, the gossip always reached him, and where that had failed, Canterbourne had been there to give him insight into Lady Godiva and her past. Marcus knew well Plumberly had jilted her a few seasons prior, and the mere thought she'd honor the earl with a dance over him was both insulting and beyond fathoming.

CHAPTER 3

*T*here wasn't a thing Godiva desired more than to call off her dance with Plumberly, especially due in part to the way he'd called off their betrothal three seasons before. She was more the lady and was loath to admit the fact to a stranger—even a dastardly handsome duke. She couldn't blame the earl for his decision, though she did hold him responsible for the scandal heaped upon her—and her family, after he'd been so brazenly seen courting another woman before they'd officially called off their betrothal. She'd been shocked when Plumberly had taken her card without a word and written his name on it this evening.

Godiva once more turned her attention to the strong shoulders and muscular legs of the duke beside her. No one would venture to give them a cruel moniker like Plumberly and Portly, as they had with her and the earl.

No, the Duke of Beargarner would likely be dubbed the bear to her Goldilocks, though no one would dare mistake her for a proper, fair-haired maiden—or him a bear. She knew nothing of the man and only had occasion to set eyes upon him this once.

He was a relative unknown to her, though she'd been comfortable enough to accept his offer of an escort on her journey back to the ballroom.

His name *was* rather fitting.

His hair hung past his shoulders, tied back with a black velvet ribbon in a nearly acceptable fashion. His intense gaze lent an almost animalistic appeal to him, though she'd never insult him by equating him to a beast. Even if she'd previously made that mistake.

What had she been thinking? The last thing she needed or *wanted* was another man. Especially not a suitable, handsome, charming man with the capacity to crush her once again. Godiva had solidly set her sights on mundane, stodgy, and possibly elderly; with no risk of giving her heart, hopes, and dreams to another, only to have them thrown back in her face when the lord decided her dowry wasn't sufficient enough or her ample figure was too off-putting.

"Shall we?" His penetrating stare asked more questions than the simple two-word inquiry implied.

Godiva hadn't realized they'd arrived at the ballroom due to the silence surrounding them. If she closed her eyes, she'd think it remained just the two of them. The room had gone silent as all eyes turned to stare at them, frozen in the doorway. Couples halted mid-step on the dance floor, the music having either ended or stopped mid-note.

Lady Godiva, the overweight, spinsterish daughter of Lord Garland, and the Duke of Beargarner, a recluse with much intrigue surrounding him, were poised as if they were the guests of honor finally arrived to greet their audience.

She laughed, a deep, throaty chuckle.

The sound echoed through the room, bounced off the walls—restarting time.

The musicians struck up the beginning notes of a waltz when she nodded in their direction. Startled, she realized they'd paused for her; she commanded this room, something she was highly unaccustomed to. She was the wallflower, the quiet lady who'd been content to watch others as they danced the night away. However, this was her home...and her family ballroom.

She spied Lady Delilah and Lord Canterbourne as they took their places on the dance floor.

Out of the corner of her eye, she saw Plumberly making his way toward her to claim his dance.

Beargarner had spotted him as well. His hold on her arm tightened a fraction as if he were loath to let her go.

Godiva was torn; she'd rather not let him go either yet aligning herself with Beargarner—or any man—was surely a mistake.

"Aw, Lady Godiva," Beargarner spoke loud enough for those closest to hear. "I believe this dance belongs to me." With effortless grace—something she'd had yet to master— he guided her down the steps into the room and straight to the dance floor, past a gawking Lord Plumberly. His arm held her close, though far enough away for them to look at one another. "How was that for taking what I want? I do fancy myself a quick study."

"You are a ready learner, Your Grace." It still begged the question of *why* he wanted to dance with her. Before long, they were twirling in the center of the floor with other couples surrounding them yet keeping their distance. "But I do believe you may have found a rival in Plumberly."

It was his turn to laugh. "When you are in my arms, it is Marcus, not Your Grace or Beargarner." He was quite adept at issuing commands. "Besides, Plumberly passed on any claim he might have had on you."

Her face flushed. Beargarner—Marcus—knew of her disgrace, yet she sensed his comment wasn't meant to be cruel or embarrass her. It was a statement of fact. Their movements about the floor heated her skin farther, and Godiva prayed he attributed her flushed cheeks to the exertion of the dance.

Godiva couldn't bring herself to look up and meet his scrutinizing stare, preferring to focus on his shoulder—broad as it was—and her dance steps instead. He'd taken command of their movements, expertly guiding them around the floor with little help from her. If she stumbled, she wondered if he'd be able to keep them both from tumbling to the floor.

Too quickly, their moment ended. Marcus released his hold on her and started toward her father.

"You are an exquisite partner," he complimented.

"Did you not believe a lady such as myself was capable of dance?" Her earlier embarrassment returned at her emboldened retort. It was possible the sight of both Canterbourne and Plumberly in the same ballroom had overloaded her poise. "I do beg your pardon, Your Grace. I meant no off—"

He halted, cutting off her apology. "Take heed your own advice, my lady. Do not apologize for demanding an answer to a question you deem of import." He gently patted her hand and began walking once more. "Besides, you move with a grace I have not seen in another woman since watching my mother dance with my father."

Her eyes snapped to meet his, leery of his continued kindness and innate interest. In her extensive experience, such things came at a steep price—usually her embarrassment.

"My Lord Duke." The voice couldn't be described as anything but congested, as if the woman were in dire need of a handkerchief and a private moment. "I am ready."

She is ready? For what?

Godiva turned to face the woman, a smile settling upon her lips in greeting. This was her home, after all, and she was

21

expected to greet each guest with the decorum befitting her status as Lord Garland's only daughter.

"Welcome..." Her greeting trailed off; her eyes unable to focus on the beauty before her. She was everything a woman of the *ton* was expected to be; tall, willowy with skin the color and texture of porcelain.

A proper English beauty.

Marcus stiffened, his hold tightening once again on Godiva's arm.

"Lady Gwendolyn." The icy flare to his words was not lost on Godiva. She wondered what claim the woman had on the duke, and why she now looked to Godiva with daggers in her eyes. "What a surprise. I was unaware you'd be attending this evening."

Godiva didn't believe that for a moment. She couldn't help but think he *did*, in fact, know Lady Gwendolyn was in attendance—and suspected he might have even promised her a dance.

She ignored Marcus's words, instead focusing her sights on Godiva. "Ah, Portly, I must have missed you at the receiving line, for I am sure your size is not missed often."

The blatant insult stung, causing her to take a step back and out of Marcus's hold. She was used to people speaking of her shapeliness, her age, and her penchant for attaching herself to rakehells, but never to her face nor in her own home.

Godiva couldn't breathe.

She scanned the room for help—anyone who would come to her aid.

Delilah, her dearest friend, was taking a sip of sherry while Lord Canterbourne laughed at something and leaned close to whisper in her ear.

Godiva's father was deep in conversation with Lord Haston and too far away to hear even if she called for him.

And she most certainly wouldn't expect Marcus to come to her rescue, especially with Lady Gwendolyn now softening her gaze and stepping into the place Godiva had vacated at his side. She appeared perfect next to him, the pair making a striking couple, the exact opposite of what Godiva looked like on his arm.

She was meant to grace the arm of a lord such as Plumberly or even aging Mr. Vanderall, but not the finely dressed, charming, and refined Duke of Beargarner.

Women like Lady Gwendolyn took that role. Many would say they *deserved* that role, earning it by virtue of their ideal beauty and seemingly unattainable poise.

Marcus shook Lady Gwendolyn's hold from his arm, so subtly no one but she and Marcus realized it happened—and he stared at her, prepared to do exactly what Godiva couldn't ask of him. He was going to rebuff the woman, which would bring them both into the spotlight. Something neither of them wanted—or needed. Godiva only sought to survive this one evening before retiring to the country to repair herself, find her purpose, and discover the life she'd always been meant to lead. A solitary life.

She searched the duke's stare, pleading silently for him to hold his tongue, if only for a few moments more, and then she'd be gone, away from everything.

"If you will excuse me," Godiva squeaked, barely loud enough for her ears.

Next, she did the only thing she could think to do in the situation—the one thing she'd sworn never to do—she lifted her skirts and fled the room. With no destination in mind, she simply kept her feet moving and prayed that everyone had not seen her mad dash up the stairs and out of the room. Or worse yet, heard Lady Gwendolyn's ghastly comment.

CHAPTER 4

arcus hadn't the time to process what had transpired before he was moving toward the staircase after Lady Godiva, keeping her in his sights as he navigated around other partygoers. If she disappeared into one of the rooms above prior to him catching up, she'd be lost to him.

Blast Gwen and her infuriating nature.

And curse him, as well. He should never have given Gwen hope they still shared any sort of relationship beyond nodding to one another at social functions.

If Lady Godiva refused to speak with him again, it would be warranted.

He'd stood there and said nothing as Gwen uttered her snide, deplorable insult. Gwen was angry with him—and his lack of interest in her—but she'd taken it out on Godiva. She knew her hurtful words no longer incited his temper or drew his attention.

Godiva hadn't deserved any of it.

Lady Godiva reached the top of the stairs and headed in the opposite direction he'd found her earlier that night. She maneuvered around a hall table with the ease of someone who'd roamed these halls since birth, while he had to concentrate not to catch the toe of his boot on the rug.

"Lady Godiva," he called as she rounded a corner. He thought he saw her glance over her shoulder, but he couldn't be sure he'd even called her name loud enough for her to hear over the sound of their footsteps or their combined, labored breathing.

Many guests had witnessed the entire encounter. He and Godiva entering the ballroom, arm in arm, their turn about the dance floor, and Gwen's subsequent harsh words. If that hadn't gained their attention, then Godiva's flight would have alerted the remaining guests to the unfolding scandal underway in their midst. He'd had no option but to follow her, to explain. This night, his first back in London, was turning out to be nothing like he'd expected.

He needed Lady Godiva, at least for the time being.

Up ahead, she entered the last door on the left before slamming it in her wake.

Slowing his pace, he inhaled deeply to catch his breath, weighing his next move. He hadn't made a single correct decision thus far, and it truly didn't matter what he chose now. He could knock softly and await her answer. Or simply barge in, demanding his entry.

If he were smart, he'd turn around and leave before it was too late. Find another way to circumvent the creditors who sought relief for the debts his father owed. Marcus would be wise to walk out the front doors without collecting his coat and not look back. Unfortunately, he was not in a financial position to invest in new evening attire.

He took another deep breath and prepared to knock on her door.

But his hand fell back to his side when sobbing echoed from within.

Now he was certain he should run. Leave the Garland townhouse, never to return. Erase all memory of Lady Godiva from his mind.

Instead, instinct set in, the need to protect her overwhelming him as his chest ached at the hollow sound of her sorrowful cries. He put his hand on the knob and turned, confirming Lady Godiva's earlier suspicions of his daftness.

The door opened wide to reveal the lady. Her back to him and her shoulders shaking as she cried into her hands.

He was the worst of creatures. He did not deserve to be let out in polite society.

Godiva hadn't deserved to be attacked in her own home —or anywhere, for that matter—while Marcus stood by mute. It was unfair of him to put her in a position that left her vulnerable to Gwen's spite.

Her crying increased.

Marcus should announce his presence and give her the opportunity to throw him from the room, save a piece of her dignity. But he couldn't bring himself to make a sound, nor could he be convinced to leave.

Rubbing his face with his hands, his decision was simple.

"Lady Godiva," he whispered so as not to startle her. Part of him hoped she wouldn't hear him, or demand he leave at once. But as had been the constant in their short acquaintance, she surprised him when she turned to face him, her hands dropping to reveal her tear-streaked face. "Please accept my deepest apologies."

"They are unneeded and unwarranted." Her words came on a heavy sigh. "They are as true as any other—in Lady Gwendolyn's eyes, at least."

"No one should treat another—"

"Alas, it is very common."

"Her words were—"

"Justified." Godiva straightened, the admission infusing

her with a new resolve. "My shortcomings are common knowledge. If society hadn't had them pointed out to them after my disastrous betrothal to Lord Danderfur, then they surely recognized them when Plumberly called off our arrangement. And still, if that didn't make me the scandalous lady of the century, then Canterbourne running off with my dearest friend, ending our season-long courtship...well, there is enough for all to know I am either cursed or have ample failings."

Marcus was aware of his good friend's brief attachment to Lady Godiva, but Canterbourne had assured him no hard feelings between the pair lingered. He was to wed Lady Delilah after all, and Godiva had been hard at work helping with the coming celebrations in honor of the newly betrothed couple.

Daniel, Lord Canterbourne, was the only person who knew Marcus's true motives for coming to London—and the idea behind the possible match between him and Godiva. His friend had gone on and on about the lady's suitability for marriage and the sure way in which the match would solve all of Marcus's financial woes.

Had Daniel misled Marcus?

"Come now, my lady," he soothed. "You are rather harsh on yourself."

"Not harsh, simply realistic, Your Grace." His heart broke for her—the finality in her tone.

Marcus had planned to use her for his own gains as well, but never did he expect to hurt her. She would ultimately garner much from their involvement: a title, his estate, and protection, and one day, a family.

A friendship—and affection—for one another could blossom.

He believed this possible more than ever now, after making her acquaintance.

"Godiva."

She sobered at his use of her given name and wiped the remaining tears from her cheeks.

"Now, that is better. Let us calm ourselves and return to the ballroom for one last dance."

"You cannot possibly seek my company when women such as Lady Gwendolyn await your return."

She had no sense of her own value, and he found himself wanting above all else to change that.

With a flourish, Marcus stepped back, bowed deeply, and offered her his outstretched hand. Much as he had in the hall earlier, though there was an immense increase in his sincerity this time. "My dearest Lady Godiva. Will you do me the extreme honor of accompanying me to the Garland Ball to dance the night away?"

His arm hung in the still air, and he dared to peek up from his lowered head.

Godiva eyed him suspiciously and made no move to take his offered arm.

"I do not bite," he said to lighten the sense of gloom. "Go on, take my arm, and make me the happiest man in all of London."

Her moist eyes narrowed with confusion.

"What is it?" he asked.

"I only now realized I do not know you—and yet, you have entered my private chamber."

They both looked about the room in unison.

Marcus hadn't been aware of his surroundings before, either, but since she'd pointed it out, he took a moment to survey the intimate area. An insight into Lady Godiva he hadn't realized he sought.

It was nothing he'd have expected of the woman.

He'd never encountered a room entirely done up in one color—not even a varying shade stuck out.

Pink, of the palest shade conceivable, surrounded him.

Upon every square inch of her personal chamber.

Her large, four-post bed was pink, covered in a pink, eyelet duvet. A wooden rocking horse sat in the far corner, also painted pink. Her washstand and chair before the hearth —pink.

And stranger yet, dolls sat atop every open surface. Hundreds of them, he would guess without having the liberty of time to count them all.

If she hadn't said this was her chamber, he'd have suspected it belonged to a child.

Marcus snapped his mouth shut. It had fallen open in wonder—or possibly horror—at the sight around him. He was utterly speechless. Entranced, yet repulsed.

"My word," he finally muttered. "Where in heavens did all this come from? And the same shade of pink? How is this possible?"

She turned a sheepish look to him, obviously embarrassed. "My father has it brought to England on his ships. In each port, the captain or his mate is sent ashore to locate something of this exact color. I have long feared many are dipped in some sort of dye, so as not to disappoint my father upon their return."

As she took in the room, trying to see it through his eyes, her despair lifted, replaced by a sense of wonder.

"And you've kept them all?"

"Why, of course." She said the words as if they were the most logical answer. "They were gifts from my father. Have you never been given a gift so special the thought of not possessing it would feel like a betrayal?"

He was dumbfounded. His own father had bankrupted the dukedom after his wife's death. With his mother's passing, his father spent large amounts of coin on various mistresses, risky business ventures, and other follies, including a gallery of seminude portraits. Marcus had been pressed to sell everything not entitled to the dukedom—except the portraits, for there weren't many willing to spend precious funds on them. If his father, or another family member, had ever given him something of value, it had been hocked to fetch whatever small amount it would bring in.

But it was something he'd never admitted to another—Gwen had only learned of it because she'd traveled to his country home with her family, and he'd been unable to keep secret the dwindling nature of his assets.

His plan, if he should succeed in marrying well, was to replenish the family's coffers and systematically replace all he'd had to sell off.

Failure was not an option open to him, for it would not only be he who suffered but all who depended on the Beargarner dukedom for their livelihood.

"I hadn't thought of matters in those terms, my lady." He hoped to one day give his family the type of treasures Lady Godiva possessed. Objects and possessions worth more than their weight in gold because of their sentimental nature.

And with Godiva's help, he would be able to.

He only needed to convince her to marry him—before the fortnight was through.

CHAPTER 5

*G*odiva walked about her room. She ran her fingers along the edge of her dressing table, patted her rocking horse, Ollie, on the head, and straightened the dress of her favored doll. This room had been her safe haven for more years than she could count. It was where she'd cried herself to sleep the day a girl called her plump at the dressmaker. She'd been only eight summers at the time, and the other child much older. What hurt the most was when the girl's mother had laughed at her daughter's remark and snickered behind her hand that Godiva should seek the expertise of a tentmaker to sew a dress large enough for her.

Oh, how Godiva had sobbed.

Her parents had gifted her a new doll the next day, the first of many.

She'd long suspected the gifts were a kind of compensation for all the horrible words they'd heard uttered about their only daughter. A means of showing Godiva she had worth and could find her own delight in life, if only she had one more pretty bauble to cover the not-so-pretty parts of herself.

Godiva treasured the gifts, nonetheless. They reminded her of her own choices in life.

While some chose to cast doubt on the character and looks of others in an attempt to mask their own ugly nature, every person had the option to be positive. To take the unfavorable and turn it into something virtuous and show kindness to others.

She'd determined long ago to do one good deed for every gift given to her by her guilt-ridden parents.

"Godiva?" The duke's words could have been whispered, they sounded so close. "You are crying again. Have I hurt you in some manner?"

She could listen to him say her name for eternity without tiring of it, so rarely had her name been issued from the lips of such a man.

She smiled. "No, you have not."

"Then it is Gwen's words that continue to upset you?"

"Lady Gwendolyn's words, London society...and the unfairness of life as a whole." She sighed. "Are you sorry you asked? I would not blame you if you turned now and departed."

"I do not think I could ever forgive myself if I left you."

In such a state, Godiva added silently to herself. Certainly, Beargarner would depart shortly, and Godiva would be forgotten just as quickly.

Many had left her and not given it a second thought, why would he be any different? Marcus hadn't any obligation to her; they weren't betrothed—nor were they friends. He'd been in the wrong place at an inopportune time, thus witnessing her humiliation. She needed him to understand he couldn't take the blame for Lady Gwendolyn. If it hadn't been her, then it would have likely been someone else.

"Please know I would not hold any ill will toward you if you did depart." She didn't trust herself to say more, for if she started, it was unlikely she'd stop until he'd heard her whole sordid past. In a way, she was not much different than her mother. Marcus began to trail her around the room, inspecting some knickknacks and touching others. She watched to see what specific items caught his notice. Would it give her insight into the man?

It was comforting to assess him when he thought her distracted by upset.

He gravitated toward the more bizarre pieces in her room, a pink-stained ivory tusk from the wilds of Africa, a rose quartz encrusted fan from India, and lastly, a hand-carved ship whittled from driftwood found in the Mediterranean Sea.

Perhaps he was an adventurer at heart; a need to explore more than London—or even England—had to offer.

She should be cautious with the man, yet his presence calmed her, especially after the incident with Lady Gwendolyn. The ease Godiva felt in his company was something she'd never experienced with Danderfur, Plumberly, or Canterbourne. It made no sense. A man she knew nothing about seemed more familiar to her than three men she'd planned to wed and at one point had seen herself in love with.

Picking up a pink pearl inlaid hand mirror, Godiva remembered the day she'd discovered Lord Danderfur's deceptions. He'd been a kind enough man, though merely a baron. She'd been drawn to him due to his sensitive nature and mild manner of speaking. His cultured appearance pleased her parents greatly. It was a mere two days before they were to be married that she'd caught him in her room—wearing the dress she'd planned to be wed in.

The whole scene would have been comical had it not happened to her—and most assuredly if her father hadn't been there to witness the debacle. It was ultimately Lord

Garland's decision to force Danderfur to call off the nuptials, though Godiva had insisted on hearing Danderfur's reasoning.

It was one of the precious moments where her father had saved her from her own naiveté. With each passing year, Godiva developed the ability to guard her own heart.

The morning after the embarrassing discovery, shortly after Danderfur had departed England for Paris, the pink mirror and matching brush had appeared in her room.

When she was younger, she'd imagined her father kept a full shop somewhere in London, loaded to the rafters with pink in preparation for the many slights Godiva would no doubt experience during her life. As she aged, she stopped wondering about the gifts and their origins. Their appearance only meant another cruel soul had set forth more negativity into the world, *her* world.

Godiva had learned long ago that under no circumstances was she to trust her instincts with men. She'd been wrong more times than she'd been right. Unfortunately, the times she was wrong always led to heartbreak. Another affront leveled on her family. Another season of her mother parading her to all the balls, recitals, plays, country picnics, and the like.

If it were her choice, she'd wed a man with all haste to finally put a stop to the never-ending cycle of overwhelming entertainment. Godiva sought only peace.

The duke's footfalls halted. "I think it past time *we* return to the ballroom."

"Of course, Your Grace," she muttered. "Many must have noticed our departure."

His stare narrowed on her. "It is not the reason I seek to return."

"Oh, it is Lady Gwendolyn." Godiva didn't want to hear his response, nor dwell on her curiosity regarding his relationship with the lady. It was none of her business if the pair were friends, or former lovers, or lovers—though, thinking of the pair as *lovers* made her envious. "You truly should make amends with her before the eve is done."

"No." At some point, Marcus had come to stand directly behind her. His hand, gentle yet rough from years of labor—which she found odd for any man of the *ton*—rested on her bare arm above her glove. She turned willingly to face him when he tugged lightly. "Because I intend to have my second dance of the evening with you."

Godiva tilted her chin up until her eyes met his—dark, rich, cocoa brown. How had she never noticed the depth that lay there, the complexity residing barely below the surface? It hinted to the intricacy that was this man. Much like the cunning bear, his namesake.

Maybe he only appeared the hunter from the outside with his long, barely restrained hair, dark eyes, and muscular frame. It was possible that was all there was to the Duke of Beargarner: an agreeable exterior with little beneath, in a similar fashion to many other noblemen of her acquaintance.

His hand hadn't left her arm but held her in place.

Her gaze drifted to his lips, parted ever so slightly as if he was prepared to say something but was hesitant to let the words escape.

She knew the feeling well, for she was doing the same. Did her lips appeal to him as much as his did to her? She rather doubted that—her lips had always been a bit too plump.

Finally, Marcus let the words slip out. "Can I kiss you?"

Godiva had longed for a moment such as this, dreamed of a man such as him, but had resigned herself to a chaste future, never knowing a magical moment. Yet, here the chance had arisen...and she feared it would never present itself again.

"I do not know, *can* you?" she breathed. Not exactly the words she'd been holding back.

The spark that lit his eyes said her words pleased him greatly. "Point taken, my lady."

His mouth captured hers swiftly and without hesitation as if he were laying siege. What he didn't realize was that she had no defenses to protect herself from his sweet attack.

She did not seek to protect herself at all but revel in the moment.

Their lips melded together, and Godiva followed his lead to territories previously unknown to her. Marcus was destined to bring her to paradise. And she would stay as long as he allowed her to.

She gripped his shoulders, mentally forcing her fingers to loosen their hold as she sank into his embrace. Her head tilted farther back as he stepped closer. He was much taller than her. The height difference shouldn't work, yet she fit against him as if she'd always been destined to stand in his embrace.

With a flick of his tongue against her parted lips, all her thoughts, questions, and concerns were thrown to the wayside. Continuing the movement, Marcus's tongue ran across her lower lip in the slowest of crusades, strategically planned to drive her mad with desire.

A desire she'd never known before.

A desire she never wanted to let escape her grasp.

A desire only Marcus could stoke within her.

She longed to cherish the duke as much as she did the gifts filling her bedchamber.

$\mathcal{L}$ady Godiva's mouth moved against his, taking all he offered as if she'd kissed many men before him. It shouldn't have been a surprise, as she'd been betrothed before. But Marcus did not wish to speculate on whom she'd kissed previously. Coils of jealousy roared through him until his neck blazed with heat. He had the urge to keep her close, hidden from any man who sought to glance upon her; it was a possessiveness unfamiliar to him.

He'd always been a man who preferred solitude—counting on no one and nothing for his survival, yet suddenly, he knew he could not live without her.

His mind was addled by her intoxicating scent, honeysuckle and...lavender.

He wrapped his arms more securely around her, bringing her ample bosom to his chest. She was delicate in his embrace, fitting perfectly within his arms. He couldn't remember another woman feeling this right.

His head screamed that he should release her before they progressed any further, but his body demanded he make her his. She wanted his touch as much as he wanted to touch her.

Reluctantly, Marcus released his hold on her and stepped back, their lips parting.

The disappointment in her stare was enough to warn him he'd made the wrong decision. Her arms wrapped around her waist, and her eyes clouded warily. A moment before, she'd been open to him, receptive to his attentions. Just as quickly as she'd stepped into his arms, her wariness returned, and he watched as a door slammed shut on her emotions, effectively closing her off.

He'd conquered her defenses, only to allow them to return stronger than before.

"Lady Godiva?"

Her fingers lifted to touch her pink, swollen lips as she gazed up at him with wonder.

Something was wrong—off in some way Marcus couldn't grasp.

He waited, fearing she would run from the room in tears, which would make the second time this night he'd caused her pain.

"My first kiss." A shy smile tugged at the corner of her mouth. "Thank you, Your Grace."

Marcus didn't know what surprised him more: that she'd never kissed another or that she was thanking him as if he'd done her a great service.

"You were right," she continued.

Marcus had never felt so amiss. About everything—his plans while in London to reverse his fortune, his past with Gwendolyn, and most assuredly, his rash decision to pursue Lady Godiva.

Maybe, just maybe, she was the one in control of the situation.

Nothing scared him more than losing what little control he had left.

"What was I right about?"

Her chin lowered as her eyes drifted to the floor at his feet. "It is time we returned to the ballroom for our dance."

Another thing he was incorrect about. Marcus wanted to stay here, surrounded by her feminine, pink room; take her into his arms once more and finish what they'd started.

There was satisfaction in the knowledge that no man had touched her before. Not Danderfur, nor Plumberly, nor Canterbourne.

Senseless rogues, the lot of them.

Each and every one had lost something truly magnificent —without even realizing it.

"Apparently, I am very wise." Marcus extended his arm for her to take in an attempt to regain his composure. "A crowded ballroom is the perfect place for us to be at this exact moment."

They made their way below, closing the door on their lost moment. Lady Godiva moved with a fluidity and grace most ladies never achieved, while Marcus strode, his stance rigid in an attempt to govern his body, aching with need. Each doorway they passed, he imagined opening, pulling her inside to steal another kiss.

A nook with a small seat cut into the wall was tucked into the space as they took the final stair to the main floor. If he positioned them just so, no one would notice them within.

Next, they passed the cloakroom where servants hurried in and out, storing guests overgarments and accessories. Most assuredly, they could disappear within the room of fabrics for a few moments without anyone the wiser.

Marcus was acting like a ruddy boy fresh from university. If Canterbourne felt any measure of what he did when he looked at—held—Lady Delilah, then he was justified in making the woman his.

But Marcus was not Canterbourne. He wasn't free to marry for love or affections, nor allowed the time it would take for such things to develop. He was an impoverished duke. Although, only a few were aware of his troubles. The fact did not make his circumstances any less severe.

Curse his father for putting him in such a sore financial position.

Curse Canterbourne for giving him the idea to restore his family's coffers.

Curse Gwendolyn for causing a scene and giving him no other option but to follow Lady Godiva.

Every eye in the room turned their way for a second time as they re-entered the ballroom. In response, he pulled Godiva closer, and her fingers tightened in the crook of his arm.

He was no stranger to being the center of attention, especially when he'd entered a room with Lady Gwen on his arm; however, having Godiva at his side was different. In a surprising way.

Marcus couldn't help but think he'd publicly announced his courtship of Lady Godiva in a far more open manner than he'd expected. If the move kept other men away, so be it.

As they took the dance floor once more, he reminded himself he was here for one thing—their marriage would be a means to acquire unregulated cargo ships to import his goods, sugar cane, tobacco, and hemp, from across the world, and in turn, gain enough coin to remain free of debtors' prison. A contract that united their families and forged a bond useful for Marcus's future business endeavors.

To accomplish his goal, he needed Lady Godiva's hand in marriage. Only her hand.

In no way did that include giving his heart to her.

Marcus steeled his resolve as he glanced down into Lady Godiva's upturned face—and just as quickly, his newly returned resolution crumbled.

"Marcus," she said. "May I ask you a question?"

When she said his name, he heard nothing else.

"Of course, Godiva."

"How is it that we've never met before this eve?"

"I do not journey to London often." It was the simplest answer which wasn't a lie.

"And yet you are here...attending a ball held in my honor."

He would surely offend her if he admitted Canterbourne hadn't thought to mention the reasoning for the ball, only that it would afford him the perfect opportunity to make her acquaintance.

"Oh, I can see you were unaware." She laughed, and he suspected it was to cover her embarrassment. "Do not fret. Many do not know this ball is my parents' final attempt at seeing their only daughter wed before her twenty-fourth birthday."

He wanted to curse his friend and Lady Delilah for their interference in his life. Nothing about the idea had to do with his financial woes and instead all to do with his personal affairs.

"May I offer you my sincere good tidings on your birth-day?" Marcus drew her close and spun her in a wide arc about the floor. "Every eye in the room is on you. I do believe Lord and Lady Garland's planning has been to your advantage."

"And how is that?" She glanced at his shoulder again, avoiding eye contact. If his hands weren't duly occupied holding her, he would lift her chin. "You have significantly occupied my time."

"If you seek the company of another—"

"No." She spoke quietly, but the single word held conviction—and he couldn't repress his smile.

She'd selected him over the other options hanging about the ballroom. Even now, a few elderly men conversed with her father, casually glanced in Godiva's direction, awaiting her return.

"It seems you have a crowd awaiting you."

Her eyes lifted, briefly glancing in her father's direction. A heavy look settled, dampening her jovial mood. "Please, do not do that."

"You do not want to make a good match?"

She settled her glare squarely on his. "Does not every lady wish for a good match?"

"I'm not asking about 'every lady,' I only inquire about you." His smile lessened. "What do you wish for your future?"

She fell silent for so long Marcus worried their conversation had come to an end. Finally, she responded, "To marry a man in good standing and provide an heir, of course."

It was the customary answer drilled into every debutante's head since birth. "No, not what you've been told to want by your family and what society deems proper for you. What do *you* want? Adventure? Love? Mayhap, a goat farm?"

"A goat farm?" She laughed. "I hadn't realized that was an option. Will my hands become dirty?"

"Positively filthy, my lady."

"What goes into one managing a proper goat farm? I am certain it is more difficult than running a household."

He stared past her to the couples swirling about them, forming his response. "Property, a large pail for feeding—and a goat or two." Marcus found he was enjoying their conversation, as unconventional as it was. "But, do not set your sights on the farm without considering your other choices."

"I would like to travel, mayhap, to see the places from which my father's men have collected all my gifts." Her words turned serious, their depth far deeper than what one normally conversed about in a crowded ballroom, but after an evening spent discussing the weather and current fashion trends, Marcus welcomed it. "I have only read of lands far away."

"You have never sailed on one of your father's ships?" He wondered if his words were genuine, or if he was only seeking further information about Lord Garland's business dealings. "I mean to say, have you been to port?"

"Oh, heavens, no," she replied. "My father would never allow me—or any female—to accompany him during his business dealings. He says it is not the proper place for those of delicate sensibilities."

"And do you always adhere to your father's wishes?" All thoughts of financial woes had vanished from his mind; his existence depended on this very conversation. Nothing else mattered but Godiva's response.

The music abruptly came to an end, and the final chord drifted through the large room before silence invaded. He'd been focused on their conversation and movement. If he'd realized how little time they had left in each other's arms—and company—he might have talked of a subject other than goats.

Which Marcus should want. Making Lord Garland's acquaintance was important and his main objective for the evening, with Lady Godiva and their introduction being second at hand. But now, he realized he wanted a few more moments with her alone—and time to finish their conversation.

Societal rules dictated he return her to her father, no matter what he desired.

"Your Grace." They drifted through the crowd toward Lord Garland. "Might I trouble you for a refreshment and a stroll about the terrace?"

"Of course." He latched on to her suggestion and changed their direction in favor of the drink table and the terrace doors a few feet beyond. "I would not be a gentleman if I allowed you to go without refreshments."

With drinks in hand, they stepped through the open doors, no one standing in their way. He couldn't help but picture them back in her room, away from the noise and activity of the ballroom.

Marcus slowed his pace, but she pulled him a bit farther into the shadows, away from the other people milling about closer to the torches posted outside the terrace doors. The conversations around them drifted on the breeze, sounding little louder than murmurs.

It was not the privacy of her chamber; however, neither were they under the watchful eye of others.

"I feel horrid for monopolizing your entire evening, Lady Godiva," he confessed. More shocking was that he actually meant the apology. Especially if Lord and Lady Garland had planned the ball specifically to find her a suitable match before the season ended. He shook his head—he desired to be that match, though Lady Godiva was unaware of his intentions. "I promise to return you as soon as you've had a spot of fresh air."

"Oh, I know everyone in attendance," she sighed. "The only exception being Lady Gwendolyn and you. How did you say you received an invitation?"

He couldn't see lying to her for the truth would surface eventually. "Lord Canterbourne insisted I attend with him. And shortly after our arrival, he sought the company of your friend, Lady Delilah." Marcus waited for her reply, unsure if she'd be upset or angry. Or if like Canterbourne had said, there were no hard feelings or resentment left. "And I am certainly pleased I accepted his offer."

"Ah, I see."

Marcus didn't doubt she saw something—but what it was escaped his understanding.

$\mathcal{L}$ady Godiva took in the plate before her, filled to overflowing with eggs, cold pheasant, and pickled pear. It never ceased to amuse her that the servants believed her proportions dictated she consumed this much at each meal. They seemed not to notice her plate went mostly untouched.

Closing her eyes, she said a small prayer before glancing at her plate once more.

She picked up her fork and turned her attention to the head of the table, where her father sat reading the morning post. Above him on the wall, Lady Godiva's portrait hung. At some point during the hours since the ball had ended, the servants had relocated it back downstairs and repositioned it behind her father on the wall. At least he would not be required to stare at the thing while he ate. It had been very wise of him to dictate the painting's newest spot before Lady Garland left her chambers.

"Godiva," he called, keeping his eyes on his paper.

"Yes, Father?"

"The gossips are saying you spent much of your evening

with a certain unknown gentleman." Lord Garland did not hover over his only child, nor question her actions or decisions.

"Yes. I did spend a bit of time with Lady Delilah but needed to assist Mother to her room when she fell ill. On my return to the ballroom, I met the Duke of Beargarner." She needn't share he'd awaited her right outside her mother's chambers. "He requested a dance, and I did not think it proper to turn down his offer."

"Beargarner..." Her father puzzled over the name. "Beargarner...I believe I knew his father long ago. Nice chap?"

Her father kept his gaze on his paper, but she wasn't fooled. He listened to her every word, and it was likely he knew more about Marcus than she did, even after spending the majority of her time with him the previous evening.

"He was a gentleman." All she could think of was his arms around her, and his lips pressed to hers. "Why do you ask?"

"I had heard word he was in town to speak with me about my cargo ships."

"What?" She didn't mean to speak aloud. Or to sound so dejected.

"Yes, he hopes to gain an agreement to transport cargo on my ships." Her father never spoke of business, either with Godiva or while she was present in a room. "It merely surprised me the pair of you are acquainted."

"Oh?" Godiva focused on her plate but continued to listen to his every word. "I wouldn't say we're acquainted. We simply danced."

"Ah, well." He cleared his throat. "I am happy you enjoyed your evening."

Godiva had thought she'd enjoyed her night immensely. Now she wasn't at all sure. Had him making her acquaintance, their dance, and their kiss all been a ploy on the duke's part?

Lord Garland shook the wrinkles from his paper, refolded it, and prepared to take his leave.

She struggled to catch her breath as she thought through every moment of the time they'd spent together.

Standing, he continued, "Your mother is still a bit unwell. She bids you keep to your activities and collect her new bonnet from the shop. Good day. I will see you at supper." And he left the room, oblivious to his words' impact on her.

Marcus was only in town to gain something from her father. It was clear he thought the quickest way to getting it was to dupe her into favoring him. Likely to prod Godiva to share with her father how kind and attentive he'd been. Had his intentions been to give Lord Garland the hope she was not confined to her shelf, but might instead surprise them all and have a duke offer for her hand?

Marcus must have feigned ignorance at the relevance of the ball to her.

In fact, he'd played his cards as well as Godiva had ever witnessed. He'd thoroughly convinced her of his good nature, caring sentiment, and manners, and as of an hour ago, she'd actually caught herself daydreaming of what life with Marcus could be like. He'd preyed on her previous history with men, knowing she'd be out of chances come a fortnight.

But what had Canterbourne's part been in it all? Marcus had admitted his invitation came from him—had they planned this scheme together with Delilah's help?

Her friend would not betray her so, though she had taken Canterbourne for herself. Before now, Godiva had actually believed her friend had saved her from a loveless marriage.

Godiva pushed her untouched plate away and stood, pacing the long room.

Her instincts with men had long been her downfall. "How *dare* he!" she seethed.

"My lady?" a footman inquired from the far end of the room. "Is your meal not to your liking? I can have Cook prepare something more pleasing to you."

She'd never be used to always having someone present. It hadn't bothered her before, but recently she'd sought time to herself, brief moments to think—which was nearly impossible with servants always on hand. "My apologies, Fetter. I am well. The meal, as always, was very pleasing. Please inform Cook I said as much." The servants cared about her, and she them, so their attentiveness wasn't meant to be invasive.

He bowed. "Of course, my lady. Do call if you require anything else."

"Actually, have the carriage readied. I will depart within the hour." She sat to put the servant at ease, yet it did nothing to dim her own anger.

"My pleasure."

Godiva was finally alone, something she thought she'd wanted, but now—with the full weight of her father's words crashing down on her—it would have been nice to have someone else present if only to keep the hurt and tears at bay.

Why her? It would have been just as easy—if not easier—to approach her father, leaving her out of their dealings altogether. Instead, the duke had cornered her above the stairs, pushed his acquaintance on her, and practically forced her to accept his offer to dance. He'd targeted her, knowing exactly who she was and what she could offer him.

Lies.

He hadn't forced her to do anything she wasn't completely willing to do.

She'd adored every moment in his arms. Every envious look turned her way by matrons and newly introduced young ladies alike. Men who'd ignored her presence only hours before had requested a spot on her dance card for future balls. On the surface, Marcus, Duke of Beargarner, was every lady's dream, titled, wealthy, charming, dashing, refined, and elegant.

He'd hidden his only fault with the expertise of a practiced liar.

London was filled to overflowing with ladies who would be willing to overlook his deception in favor of becoming a duchess.

His duchess.

Despite her past follies, she was not that woman any longer.

Godiva knew the mistrust and confusion of being betrayed by a man—or three.

She pushed her chair back, the wooden legs scraping the floor so loudly, she feared it would draw a servant to the room. Confident she would remain alone, Godiva stood and paced the room.

Danderfur had made his intentions known only days after her presentation...and asked for her hand just shy of two months later. Godiva had thought herself one of the luckiest debutantes of the season; though only a baron, Danderfur came from a long line of respectable and responsible men—and it hadn't escaped her notice that he always dressed in the height of fashion. Her affection for him had been extinguished the day she caught him prancing in her private chamber wearing her wedding gown.

And the Earl of Plumberly—he'd had to work harder for her notice. Nearing the end of her third season, she'd relented and allowed him to take her for a ride in Hyde Park. Not a soul would be able to find a comparison between him and Danderfur, for he was rounded in size and socially inadequate, but kind and very attentive. He'd been shy to the extreme on that first carriage ride, and she'd instantly gone against her pledge and took a liking to him—and he to her, she was sure. But then the name-calling started. "Plumberly is to wed Portly" was the exact title in the gossip rag. She'd cried for days over the mean-spirited article. Her mother had assured her the earl had most likely not seen the periodical and was above such gossip.

But, alas, he'd called off their betrothal not long before they were to wed.

The only people it hurt more than Godiva were Lord and Lady Garland.

They were happy—and normally oblivious to all that happened outside their home.

Instead of focusing on her own recovery after the scandal, Godiva had had to contend with her mother's increased bouts of hysterics and alternating melancholy. Her father, in a drastically uncharacteristic change, had finally set his mind to avenging her honor by calling to task all the men who'd wronged his beloved daughter.

She'd been refused the time she needed to heal in favor of showing a brave face to her parents.

Godiva cried not only for herself but for them.

The memory alone was enough to bring a fresh round of tears to her eyes.

She halted her pacing and tilted her head back, hoping they'd disappear. Instead, they fled the corners of her eyes and moved down her cheeks. She dashed them away, allowing her anger to ignite.

She should have known that Canterbourne was responsible for...for *all* of this.

He'd led her to believe he would offer for her hand last season. He had accompanied her to the opera, escorted her and her family to Lord Chartwright's country party, and taken her for rides all over fashionable London proper. Imagine her parents' horror when they stumbled across

Canterbourne and Godiva's dearest friend, Lady Delilah, in a tender embrace. Of course, Godiva had rushed to her friend's defense, despite the pain and shame it'd caused her.

The wounds were still fresh, though she didn't see the positive aspect of dwelling on Canterbourne's deception, except where it played into Beargarner and his motives.

Again, she hadn't listened as her intuition had told her to run, put Marcus and his handsomeness far from her mind.

Trusting beauty had never benefited her.

Trusting kindness had most certainly never benefited her.

And trusting a man's actions and words had been the worst.

What had led her to believe a man possessing all three at once would garner her a different outcome?

Maybe women were the inferior species, as so many believed. They were led by their emotions—a fatal flaw if Godiva had ever encountered one.

It took her back to her original question, why her? Out of all the ladies in society, why her? He had women like Lady Gwendolyn lusting after him. Why pick an overweight, aging spinster to pursue?

Something else must have motivated him, drove him to set his sights on her, for his attention could in no way be random or unplanned. Or she was dealing with a far more sophisticated man than she'd thought possible.

He'd entered her room, her childish chamber, and touched her things.

Her cheeks heated at what else he'd touched—with his lips. It could be why she'd thought his intentions all the more serious.

It had been her first kiss, and glorious—unexpected as it had been.

Now, that memory would be forever tainted by his ruse.

Danderfur had never touched her—and now she knew

his secret, as he'd departed England with Sir Yardley shortly after he called off their engagement. Plumberly had been too wary and apprehensive in his courtship to kiss her. And Canterbourne had obviously been dreaming of lips that did not belong to Godiva.

But Marcus...he'd seized the first opportunity presented to take her mouth, laying claim to her as no lord ever had. And she'd allowed him. More than that, she'd pressed against him in the most wanton of manners. She hesitated to ponder what further liberties she'd have allowed him had he only spoken his request.

At the time, it had seemed he'd wanted her for his own. Broken past the barriers she hadn't realized were there to claim what he desired. The emotions she'd felt were unlike anything she'd allowed herself to feel before.

And Marcus had stolen such bliss back quicker than he'd given it.

Trade. Business dealings. Cargo transport.

Why had she allowed herself to linger on the notion she was actually worth any more than that?

She wasn't willowy, fair, and breathtakingly beautiful like Lady Gwendolyn.

She wasn't dark-haired with enchanting blue eyes and a large dowry like Delilah.

And she most certainly wasn't a gentleman like Sir Yardley.

Maybe her worth lay only in what she could offer in business dealings. It was no different than two well-titled families pushing their offspring to wed and effectively merging fortunes and landholdings.

But it did not make the idea, or her future, any less depressing.

"My lady?" She turned to find her footman standing mere feet from her. "Your carriage awaits."

She nodded, not trusting herself to speak.

The thought of sulking about the house for days on end while she wallowed in self-pity was not an option this time. She was past allowing another to make her feel rejected, devalued, and devoid of worth.

She'd said "never again" after the last time.

The day must continue as she'd planned, without further thought of that scoundrel Beargarner. No more would she think of him as Marcus. *That* man no longer existed. Never had existed; she corrected her thinking. He was a sham. A concocted farce she'd readily accepted.

An excursion to the dress shop, a quick stop at the book-store, and finally, a visit to the local rug importer. They were all places her mother frequented, but Godiva was experienced enough to make the trip on her own. It would keep her mind duly occupied. For the afternoon, at least.

CHAPTER 8

*M*arcus had an aching head. Odd as he hadn't imbibed a single sip of liquor the previous evening. Despite the throbbing, he'd committed to meeting Canterbourne and Lady Delilah for an afternoon meal, the pair likely using him as a chaperone.

Regardless, he needed to eat—and Canterbourne's town-house was lightly staffed for being the residence of a marquis. He didn't relish overtaxing the staff so early in his stay.

He'd dragged himself out of bed at an ungodly hour, called for a bath—which turned out to be lukewarm water in a basin not large enough to bathe a small hound dog—and dressed quickly to catch Daniel before he left to meet Lady Delilah.

Now, he sat in a small eatery, staring at his friend as they waited for Lady Delilah to arrive. He'd purposely chosen the seat backed into the corner to allow Daniel a spot of privacy, but it also gave him a full view of the establishment, including the door leading in and out. One never knew when one would need to make a hasty departure.

Marcus knew an inquisition awaited him, though he was able to do naught about it.

And it wasn't just his friend. It was likely Lady Delilah would demand to know what transpired between Marcus and Godiva.

He loathed sharing any morsel of information about his time with Godiva; she'd been a surprise, to say the least. She was everything he hadn't expected—kind, witty, and...well, her lips! The draw to keep Godiva for himself was strong.

He'd been prepared to find her a simpering, spoiled maid with a mind only for fashion and pretty things. Given a life of privilege, and in such fashion, expecting others to treat her thusly. It was with great disbelief—and elation—that he'd found her to be nothing of the sort. She had a caring nature he hadn't witnessed in another in many, many years.

Canterbourne had prepared him to meet a lady of advanced age—being in her fifth season—with excess pounds about her middle, a forthright nature, and mousy, uninspiring looks. His friend must get his hearing and sight looked over by a physician, as he'd significantly underestimated everything pertaining to Godiva.

He couldn't move past the magic that had sparked between them, utterly unexpected, yet not unwelcome. He'd hardly thought of another thing all night, which likely caused his sore head today.

He'd never expected to find a soulmate, someone he could envision his life with. Yet, his draw to Godiva was undeniable. Her inner—as well as her outer—beauty drew him in, speaking to his very soul.

In their short time together, they'd formed a bond like no other he'd ever experienced. He'd spent the entire night dissecting their meeting, their words, their kiss—looking for something, anything to explain it all. He'd come to the realization it just *was*.

And that was enough for now.

It had to be.

He'd been alone for the majority of his life, deprived of another who understood him. The endless days and nights had stretched before him for so long, they ran into each other with nothing distinctive or changing. But he knew with a deep-seated knowledge there was more to life. There had to be more. At least for him.

It seemed to be much the same for her, and that was enough to bond them, though she may not yet recognize it.

"You are quiet," Canterbourne observed, picking a speck of lent off his coat sleeve.

"I have much on my mind and even more at risk." Merely speaking about it lifted some weight from him. Hiding the truth had become too much to bear, burying the depression deep inside of him where it was unlikely anyone would ever uncover it. "It is only a matter of time before my father's creditors discover I am residing at your townhouse."

Daniel's brows drew high. "That does not mean I will allow them entrance."

He admired his friend's willingness to assist him. "I wish it were that simple."

"Have you stopped by your townhouse or sent word you are in town?"

"Bloody hell, no," Marcus sighed, sinking farther into the corner as his headache increased, pounding at his temples and behind his eyes. "I swore to myself when I return there—or to the country estate—I will have things worked out. My servants are worried they will not have a post shortly."

"They know of your troubles?" Daniel asked.

"Of course," he confessed. "How could I not tell them? They knew my father's weaknesses, and, just like me, they noticed the creditors arriving in droves a few years back. I had to tell them. Thankfully, they are a loyal bunch, and as far as I know, haven't let out my upcoming ruin."

"I hadn't realized how dire things were. I am sorry for that." Canterbourne clasped him on the shoulder. "Though I have been otherwise preoccupied as of late, that is no excuse for allowing you to face all this unassisted. I can lend you all you need."

"The last thing I would ask of you is to align with my downfall this close to your nuptials. Besides, I am heavily indebted, far beyond even my wildest imaginings. I could never ask you to dig me out."

"Then, what?" his friend asked, shrugging his shoulders, belying the severity of the situation Marcus faced. "You will scrape your way out or resign to debtor's prison, when I have the means to help?"

"I appreciate a place to lay my head at the moment—and we are not only friends due to the deepness of your pockets."

"My dashing good looks?"

Marcus eyed Canterbourne with a mock look of repulsion. The marquis was elegant, charming, and his handsome looks were rather dashing, what with his clear blue eyes and blond locks, but far be it for Marcus to admit that. "They are adequate, or so I've heard."

His friend had been the target of every marriage-minded matron since before he hit his majority. Many had set their sights on him, including Godiva at one time, yet Lady Delilah had captured his heart—officially calling off the hounds.

"Do remember, I am willing to help."

"For now, thank you for allowing me to stay at your home, and for keeping my presence quiet." Marcus hadn't many friends he counted on as family. It was reassuring to know Daniel would be there, even if it were only for weekly visits at Newgate, where he'd likely end up if he weren't able to secure a marriage to Lady Godiva.

"I assume last night went well?" Daniel moved to a topic much more agreeable to Marcus. "I hardly caught a glimpse of you, except when you entered the ballroom with Lady Godiva on your arm."

"Why didn't you tell me it was a celebration for her birthday?"

"Oh, come now. That isn't until next week. Besides, it wouldn't have made any difference."

"It still would have been preferable to know." Marcus scowled at his friend. "I felt like a dolt."

"You are only pursuing the chit for her father's ships and an expedited means of restoring your coffers," Canterbourne said, his brow furrowing in exasperation. "Do not act overly invested."

Marcus remained quiet, knowing it would be foolish for him to admit he'd thought of nothing else but Godiva since leaving her the night before. If he were lucky, everything would end with him tied to "the chit" for the remainder of their years. He chose instead not to insult Daniel by pointing out his mistakes in regard to Godiva.

"Be that as it may, it would have endeared me to her if I'd known and bestowed good tidings." As an afterthought, he continued, "And she isn't simply 'some chit' to you."

Marcus fancied Daniel a man in love, ever so blinded by it he was unaware of the destruction he'd caused when pursuing his own lady fair. Marcus wasn't sure he could live with the knowledge his friend had injured another without a second thought to her feelings—or that Lady Delilah could cause such hurt to her own friend. Beneath Daniel's affectations, and despite his good fortune at finding his match, Marcus suspected he was ashamed of the way things had ended between Godiva and him.

"Ah." Veering away from any discussion on his possible past feelings for Godiva, Daniel turned to watch his ladylove enter the room, leaving her maid behind in her haste to reach his side. "Lady Delilah, I am pleased to see you once again."

Daniel stepped to her, gently laying his hand against her cheek and whispering something in her ear too softly for Marcus to hear. The couple was much in love—far beyond the formality of this meal. Marcus took in the sight of Lady Delilah while the pair was focused on one another. She was all Lady Godiva wasn't. Delilah had hair like the darkest silk, eyes of the deepest blue, and her curves were slight.

But they didn't hold a candle to Godiva—for it was Godiva's inner light that shone brighter than the sun and was more appealing than any pretty smile.

Delilah hadn't uttered a word of import during Marcus's acquaintance with her. In contrast, Godiva had said more noteworthy things within the first five minutes of their meeting.

Her supple curves only added to her appeal in Marcus's opinion. Not an inch of her was frail, nor was her disposition dour or lacking.

He could not, *would* not, admit this to Daniel. They'd been friends long enough for the marquis to see right through the front Marcus showed. He liked Godiva—more than that, he saw a future with her, beyond his financial windfall from their marriage.

The previous night he'd dreamed of things he never thought could be his. Love. Family. A home.

He'd long held that his father—and the elder Beargarner's careless ways—had stolen any possibility of those things from Marcus.

After his mother's death, his father turned to the attention of others to supplement what he'd lost. For many years, Marcus had shied away from relationships that he suspected could turn to anything more than a mutual use of one another. He'd seen the devastation his father lived through after he lost his true love, and he wasn't sure he'd do any differently if faced with that fate.

As much as he told himself he was stronger, more capable, his resistance greater; Marcus hadn't wholly convinced himself of that fact.

And he knew for certain that any attachment to—and subsequent loss of—Lady Godiva could send him spiraling in the same direction as his father.

The conversation between Daniel and his betrothed had waged on without his input or participation. Talk of the actual nuptials, blue flowers or pink? Garden ceremony in the country or more public church presentation?

Marcus was uninterested and foolish for thinking he needed food so desperately that he should accompany them. His time would have been better spent nursing his headache in bed. Which brought to mind visions of Godiva's bed...and them in it.

He shook his head to clear his wayward thoughts before they took hold of his body and presented themselves in an embarrassing, physical way.

Besides, he'd only been included by Canterbourne to lend a respectable light to the pair's meeting. He would not be called upon to interact in any sort of comprehensible way. It was possible Canterbourne and Lady Delilah would forget his presence altogether.

He weighed his options for escape, eyeing the door, when a familiar form walked by. Luckily, Delilah had also seen her and leaped from her seat to chase her down.

Lady Godiva, dressed in the palest of pinks, paused before the open door when Delilah called her name and rushed over to greet her.

The smile Godiva turned on her dear friend had Marcus jealous it was not meant for him. The ladies briefly hugged, and Delilah motioned inside to the table he and Canterbourne sat at, awaiting their repast. Godiva barely glanced inside before shaking her head no and gesturing the way she'd been walking.

Lady Delilah nodded her head as she grabbed her friend's hands, tugging her toward their table.

With one last futile look down the street, Godiva shrugged and stepped inside, Delilah pulling her along. Both men jumped to their feet when the women arrived before their table.

Marcus swayed on his feet as his headache throbbed.

Godiva addressed Daniel quickly, "My lord."

"What a grand treat, Godiva," Delilah gushed. "We were only just discussing you, and then there you were. I do believe I conjured you from thin air." Delilah took her seat next to Canterbourne as Godiva remained standing. "Do sit and have tea with us before you run off."

"I have much to do, but one cup won't hurt," she conceded. "I have been shopping for what seems like hours."

Marcus frowned when she didn't so much as acknowledge his presence.

Both he and Canterbourne regained their seats once she accepted hers.

"It is a pleasure to see you again, Lady Godiva," Marcus stated.

Her eyes snapped to meet his as if seeing him for the first time, and her look would have certainly scorched, had she had the ability to set fire with a mere glance.

"Your Grace," she said. "It is a pleasure to see you again, as well."

Marcus sensed she didn't mean the sentiment at all. Did his presence with Daniel and Lady Delilah anger her?

"Lady Godiva, I am afraid Delilah and I must hear your thoughts on flowers." Canterbourne must have also noticed the frosty tone in her greeting. "I insist Delilah's dark hair would look best with blue flowers, while she is set on pink."

"Oh, Lady Godiva will most certainly choose pink." Marcus jumped into the conversation with a conspiratorial glance at Godiva. They'd shared their first secret.

Defeated, she didn't even peek in his direction.

He took pleasure in knowing not even Canterbourne was privy to their secret. "Am I correct?"

"I most assuredly would not pick pink for your special day, Delilah." She refuted his words and shook her head firmly. "In fact, blue would be just the thing." With that, she turned to him with a smirk.

"I do not know," Delilah continued. "If we decide to wed in the gardens at Canterbourne Manor, then blue flowers would be best. But I am still not set on traveling to the country so soon after the next season starts."

"My dear." Marcus noticed Godiva cringe at Daniel's use of endearments for his intended. "I assure you people will come, no matter the time of year." Adding to both his and Godiva's discomfort, Daniel reached across the table and squeezed Delilah's hand affectionately.

"Ah, well, now that *that* is all settled, I really must go."

"But our tea hasn't even arrived," Delilah whined. "You really must stay…I need you."

Their close friendship puzzled Marcus. They made an unlikely duo. It was easy to see why Delilah was drawn to Godiva, but the reverse left him baffled. Most of his encounters with Daniel's betrothed bordered on annoying with a bit of exasperation thrown in. He must remember to ask Daniel how the two women became friends.

Godiva stood, not having been persuaded to stay as Delilah's arguments fell on deaf ears.

Marcus jumped to his feet. "I will walk you out, my lady."

"That is not necessary." Godiva waved her hand in dismissal. "My maid is waiting just outside."

"I insist." He wanted to question her about what he'd done to upset her, but he'd be damned if he'd do it in front of Daniel and Lady Delilah. "I can make sure you get to her safely and still return before our meal arrives." He moved to her side before she could protest further.

He knew the moment she gave in to his offer, for she said a quick farewell to Delilah, nodded to Daniel, and turned toward the door without taking his offered arm.

Like a puppy, he followed in her wake.

"Good luck, old chap!" Daniel laughed behind him.

Marcus had no doubt he'd need far more than luck where Lady Godiva was concerned.

CHAPTER 9

*G*odiva would have no luck at all if it weren't for her horrid luck. She'd thought her day could not possibly get any worse. Then she'd heard Delilah call for her where she sat nestled between Lord Canterbourne, and none other than the duke.

The current object of her scorn.

And then to be drawn into Delilah and Canterbourne's discussion on their upcoming nuptials. She could not conceive a worse fate, besides Marcus—the Duke of Beargarner, she corrected herself—insisting on accompanying her on her afternoon errands. Which, indeed, seemed to be occurring at that very moment. She wished the ground below her would open and swallow her whole—or better yet, open and take the *duke*.

She wasn't prepared to speak with him; the sting from their previous encounter still fresh.

Maybe she'd imagined the entire calamity from the evening before, starting with his appearance in the hallway, their kiss, their dances, and finally, their turn about the terrace? Would he declare she'd read too much into his actions, as Canterbourne had?

"Godiva," Marcus called after her.

She sped up, hoping he'd realize she was actively avoiding him and return to the inn, but he was quickly one step behind her. Why had her good sense abandoned her last night?

"Please, slow down. You are likely to turn an ankle on the uneven ground."

She stopped and pivoted to face him, a biting retort on the tip of her tongue

He stopped short to avoid colliding with her.

Godiva's glare narrowed on the man, even as she avoided focusing on his handsome face, his strong shoulders, or the pronounced way his trousers expertly showed off the muscles of his thighs. "Oh, you fear for my well-being now?"

Pedestrians detoured around them as they continued to block the walk outside her mother's favored modiste shop.

Godiva wanted nothing more than to check in with the modiste before continuing down the row of storefronts to the millinery, collect her mother's new bonnet, and return home. Once there, she could sift through everything that'd transpired between her and the duke, dissect his every word and action—while attempting to forget the alluring arrogance of his stance—and hopefully come to terms with the fact that she'd been duped once more. There must have been some clue she'd missed that pointed to his true intentions.

Whoever thought the turn of a pretty face had merely been a guise used by those of the feminine variety most certainly had not the experience of meeting lords who resided in London.

"What has gotten into you?"

"Do not act the fool, *Your Grace*," she seethed. "It is most unbecoming on you."

"Can we step inside?" He gestured to the shop behind him, the same place she'd been headed, and whose occupants were currently gazing out the window with abject interest. "Please. I promise, a quick word, and I shall depart."

Godiva glanced around as others stared as they passed the halted couple. Lord Plumberly gaped at them out of his open carriage as he rolled past, an unknown redhead accompanying him. Then Godiva looked back to Madame Isabella's and decided the modiste shop was preferable to causing a scene on the busy London street. She'd had her fill of scandals over the past few years, enough to last her a lifetime.

"Oh, drat! Fine. A moment, that is all." She stalked inside, effectively pulling her arm from his grasp. "Madame Isabella, may I trouble you for the use of your back room for a moment?"

The woman looked knowingly at Godiva before shooing her assistants to the front of the shop. Always accommodating, yet never discreet. "It is at your disposal, my lady."

"The duke and I will only need a moment to *speak*." She was sure the second they entered the backroom, Madame Isabella would send word through the servants to every shop on Bond Street about Lady Godiva and her latest beau, detailing their every word eavesdropped from her station in the front shop. She only hoped there was time for her to set the record straight before word made the rounds to her mother. "Thank you."

She pivoted toward Marcus as soon as the drapes fell shut to block their presence from the other shop patrons, her fury compounding internally ever since the discussion with her father that morning. "You cannot fathom the gossip you have started, Your Grace," she hissed in an attempt to keep her voice low. However, it rose with her ire.

"Would that be so awful?" he asked.

"Oh, you!" She stumbled on her words as she attempted

to organize her thoughts. "Of course. It would be most terrible."

His brow rose. "I was unaware our association would not be to your liking."

"Nothing about you is to my liking." She sounded like a petulant child throwing a tantrum.

"Would it not have been wise to state that before we danced—twice—last night?"

"That was before your despicable intentions were brought to my attention."

"My despicable what?" he stuttered. "What in the bloody hell do you speak of?"

"Aha!" She pointed her finger at him. "Your ill-repute is evident by your profanity in the presence of a lady."

"Do not point your finger at me," he said, standing his ground despite her anger. "And unless you truly do want a scandal, please lower your voice."

Godiva took a deep breath to calm her racing heart. She hadn't realized how loud her words had been, and she didn't doubt their confrontation would be the talk of the town within hours. Once again, her personal life—and failures—would be fodder for all of society to mock.

She wasn't even certain why she was so upset. The plan had been to simply never see the insufferable man again. But how was she to avoid him when he seemed insistent on inserting himself into her life? Delilah was *her* friend, and she might have an aversion to Lord Canterbourne, but he also belonged to her. Belatedly, she realized how peculiar that sounded, even to herself. She couldn't expect Marcus, or anyone else for that matter, to understand.

"Was the scene with Lady Gwendolyn contrived by the pair of you?"

His eyes widened, causing her to doubt her accusation.

"You are making no sense."

"But you do not refute it?" Godiva prodded. She was fairly used to men acting the fool or outright denying what she knew to be true. It was a form of manipulation she'd come to know all too well.

"There is nothing for me to refute," he sighed, throwing his arms out to the side in exasperation. "Never would I set out to hurt another person in that manner, especially you, Godiva."

But hurt her he had, with her name on his lips adding an extra slice of pain.

His trickery would not work on her again. "Especially not me. Why, because I'm your leverage for gaining a whole fleet of cargo ships? Just envision your financial windfall if you wedded Lord Garland's only portly, spinster daughter—he'd likely give you control over his amassed empire for taking me off his hands."

"Do not speak of yourself in such a fashion."

"Why?" she continued to badger him, wagging her finger in his face once more. With each step she took toward him, he retreated. "Is it not how all of the *ton* sees me? Nothing more than chattel to be traded and bartered. And a particularly large piece of chattel at that."

Her father would turn a severe look on her if he ever heard her speak such of herself—or his actions as her father. She was confident Lord Garland would never use her for his own gain, nor allow another to do so. If anything, it was he who'd always calmed her after her betrothals went to the wayside, insisting no man—lord or otherwise—with untrue intentions would ever gain her hand in marriage.

"You are so much more." His lips pressed into a firm line.

"Save your meaningless lies."

"Godiva—"

"*Lady* Godiva," she corrected. "You, Your Grace, are to

address me as 'Lady Godiva.' We are neither family nor friends."

He turned, pacing the long, narrow room. "I cannot begin to understand what changed from last night to now."

"Did you not expect me to find out that you planned to wed me for the use of my father's business investments?"

From his stunned—and ashamed—expression, he *hadn't* expected her to find out, or at least not until after they'd wed. She was but a silly chit, after all. No woman could possibly possess the sense to know when a man sought to take advantage of them. Some would say she should feel blessed to have attracted the notice of a man such as the duke, even if it was not her he was interested in.

The situation was ludicrous. As of twelve hours ago, Godiva hadn't known of the duke's existence—and now she was ensconced with him in the back room of the most popular modiste in London.

"How...who...?"

"Did you think me aged enough, large enough not to care why a handsome, titled man would seek me out?" Godiva cringed and had the urge to buy herself something pink. "I may be a mere female, but I am not a simpleton."

Marcus stopped across the room, sinking to the lounge against the wall. "Please, come sit and allow me to explain."

"I cannot," she sighed. And she couldn't...if she stayed and listened to his reasonings, he might likely fool her again with his honey-coated words and charming grin.

And she would be a fool if she believed him.

CHAPTER 10

*M*arcus could do nothing but watch Godiva walk out of the room. He listened as the bell over the front door of the shop chimed when she fled. He wouldn't chase her. The situation had spiraled out of control quicker than he could handle.

The worst of it was that every accusation she'd made was correct—or at least it had been before he'd actually made her acquaintance.

Yes, he'd expected her to be smitten with him.

Yes, he'd anticipated a girl with no prospects.

Yes, he'd planned for them to be wed before she caught on to his devious intentions.

And most importantly, yes, he'd hoped to settle his father's debts with the collectors before Godiva, or her father, became aware of his dire circumstances.

He hadn't counted on Godiva being...well, anything more than a means to attaining his much-desired ends. It was her right to lash out at him, question his integrity; at the moment, he questioned it too.

He'd made a mess of the whole situation.

Standing, he departed the shop under the watchful eye of the modiste, returned to the inn, and slumped into his seat at the table with Daniel and Lady Delilah, who'd already finished their meal and were talking quietly, their heads tilted together.

His plate sat untouched, forgotten and certainly cold before him.

"How did you fair?" Daniel asked. "She did not look pleased to see you."

"Ah…" He paused. "It is clear that she has no interest in seeing me again."

"Oh, my dear Godiva," Delilah wailed. "I should go to her. You men do know how to injure a woman."

Before either man could challenge her statement, she'd fled her seat, her reticule in hand.

Marcus had little ground to correct Lady Delilah or her opinion of him.

"Why did you ever convince me this scheme would work?" Marcus asked his friend.

"Me? I only stated marrying her would solve your problems quicker than any other solution." Daniel paused, popping the last piece of cheese into his mouth before continuing, "Besides, I cannot be held responsible for you mucking up the situation, now can I?"

"Why Godiva?" Marcus eyed the man across the table. He'd never truly thought about what his friend gained from his potential union with the lady. "Especially with your sordid past with her?"

For the first time—ever—Daniel looked sheepish, and Marcus wondered if he'd get his answer.

"It's simple. I was not looking to wed when Lady Godiva and I became acquainted. Her demeanor was likable, and I thought us gaining a friendship, of sorts."

"Go on," Marcus prodded.

As Marcus sat forward in his seat, Daniel leaned back. "She is a sweet girl. Had I not spied Delilah and instantly become smitten with her, I would have likely pursued Godiva, in time."

Marcus couldn't believe it.

"I wanted to make some kind of amends—even if she didn't know it was me—by pushing you two together."

"Then why not just tell me that?" Marcus pushed his chair back, preparing to leave. "Why the ruse with her father's shipping endeavors?"

"Because that would benefit you," Daniel said quickly. "I hadn't thought you in the market for a bride—wealthy or not. I knew your need to secure a contact within the shipping trade and thought that enough to pique your interest and bring you 'round to meeting Lady Godiva."

Marcus clenched his fist to keep himself seated. "You thought that introducing me to Godiva—and let me tell you, any man would be blessed to have her as his bride—wouldn't be enough?"

Marcus couldn't blame his friend for thinking she would fall short of what Marcus would expect in his duchess. He would never have believed it possible to meet another who so completely made him feel whole—and in such a short time.

The thought of her leaving his life devastated him.

And any man who would overlook her uniquely alluring person was the true fool.

"Understand this, Marcus," Daniel said, "I feel horrible about the way things turned out last season. I embarrassed her before society—no matter I hadn't intended to. Delilah cares deeply for her friend, and I do not want to think of myself as a man so low I'd damage a woman's good name without an afterthought."

It was the most forthright and genuine thing Daniel had

ever shared with him. And like it or not, Marcus had to accept it and make things right with Godiva.

His own pride demanded that much, even if she decided in the end she wanted naught to do with him. It was her choice, but he couldn't let her go on thinking his actions—and their kiss—had been a ploy or were in any way meant to hurt or embarrass her. He'd been genuinely attracted to her.

"Canterbourne," Marcus said, moving away from the table. "Let us be off. We have a situation to right and a lady's feelings to restore."

"We?" His friend did not appear ashamed, nor shocked, but terrified.

"Do not try to wrestle your way out of this one," Marcus called as they headed for the door and the coach that waited a short way down the street. "Though I ruined your great plan, you also owe Lady Godiva an apology—and if you could put in a kind word for me, that would be appreciated."

"I highly doubt an apology from me will mean much to Lady Godiva," Daniel argued.

"That may be so, however, we both owe her one."

Marcus hadn't any idea how she'd arrived on Bond Street, or how she got home. His only hope to address this now was to hedge his bets on Lady Delilah and her ability to waylay her friend long enough for the two slow-witted men in their lives to catch up and do the honorable thing.

The walk was busy as they made their way toward the carriage.

"Look for them," Marcus called. "They could not have gone far in such a short time."

"Ha! Women travel faster than the speed of London gossip, old chap." Daniel stopped, taking in the constant flow of people around them, none slowing or paying them any mind. "I fear there is nothing else we can do today. Can I interest you in a game of cards at White's? Your luck is so horrendous I might just win enough coin from you to cover all the food you've been eating during your stay."

"I am not prepared to give up so easily." If someone would've asked Marcus a day or two before, he'd never have thought he'd be chasing a couple of ladies about London before noon.

Alas, here he was.

And here Godiva wasn't.

"Oh, there is Lady Delilah and her maid." Daniel moved through the crowd, reaching her a moment before Marcus.

Marcus looked over the heads of the passing people in the direction Delilah had come from, but he didn't spot Godiva anywhere.

"I was too late," she said. "I am sorry, Your Grace. I do not see her carriage and Madame Isabella said she did not return to the shop. I picked up her mother's bonnet for her." Delilah lifted the box from her side.

Marcus was disappointed, not in Lady Delilah or Daniel's interfering ways, but in himself. He was foolish to think he could solve his troubles so easily and without consequences.

CHAPTER 11

*G*odiva hid her red, tear-swollen face when she departed her carriage and made her way swiftly to her chamber. Once in the safety of her room, she let the tears fall. With each sob, the anguish grew instead of lessening, ripping apart what little was left inside. Her grief wasn't all due to Marcus's deception, but the dishonesty of every man she'd ever thought to love—even if none had realized the possibility.

Leaning her back against the closed door, her willpower to stay upright gone, she slid to the floor and wept into her open palms.

Her extreme sorrow over the situation perplexed her. She and the duke had merely danced—and shared a brief kiss. The notion it would lead to anything more was childish thinking on her part. Maybe she hadn't learned as much as she'd thought from her disastrous past if it were that easy for another man to fool her.

Her chest heaved with each wretched exhale until there should be nothing left, her energy spent, yet the sobs continued unabated. Her limbs became heavy, and her eyelids lowered.

Godiva was exhausted, not only from the crying but also from life. When she was surrounded by those who cared about her, the pressures of life were held at bay. She could convince herself she wasn't ostracized by society, an outsider because of her looks. A pariah amongst those she'd always viewed as her counterparts.

She wondered what she'd done to deserve all the heartache and trickery levied upon her.

Delilah had found her perfect match without truly trying, as had every girl from Godiva's first season. Most had wed before their nineteenth birthday and now had families of their own.

Husbands, children—lives and the future to look forward to.

But not Godiva, never Godiva.

She was alone.

She glanced up to where her four-poster bed stood across the room. It seemed unreachable...miles away. But she had to make it there.

With enough sleep, maybe it would be possible to go on, start over. Although she dreaded the thought.

It was her hope that her parents would soon allow her to retire to the country for some peace, pursue things she enjoyed. Most assuredly not goat farming, but something with animals would be nice.

Above the white-and-pink eyelet spread, with the pink posts of her bed rising on each side hung the portrait of her great ancestor, Lady Godiva.

Her mother must be in better spirits to have moved the painting since the morning meal.

The urge to laugh at the sight, as was her habit when she

discovered each time the portrait was moved to a new wall, did not come.

Silently, she wondered if the great woman had let her size, and the misfortune of being wed to such an abdominal man, dictate her life. Did she shy away from society because of her circumstances? Did her people blame her for the treatment they received at her husband's hand?

Bracing her hands on the floor, Godiva pushed to her feet, determined not to live her life as society dictated—or expected.

Enough.

She'd been through this before—more than once—and she would do it again. Crying had never gained her anything but a blotchy, swollen face...and yet another pink trinket.

Movement caught her eye as she made her way to bed.

"Hello?" Godiva called, keeping a watch on her dressing room door—the door she could have sworn moved a moment before. "Is someone there?"

She should call a footman to check, yet what if it was only a rodent? The potential embarrassment kept her from shouting. Many people already thought her helpless and brainless. It was time she took care of something without depending on another.

Her parasol leaned against her washstand, placed there two nights previous. She snatched it and held it high above her head, inching toward the partially opened door; the only sound her heavy breathing.

"Is someone in there?" If someone were there, they wouldn't answer, nor could a mouse speak.

With the toe of her boot, Godiva nudged the door wide and peered inside.

The small amount of light given off by the candle on her washstand didn't reach far into the dressing-closet, but she could see something—or someone—crouched in the back corner.

"I am armed," she whispered. "Come out, or I will come in swinging!"

Which was rather absurd since she'd much rather run screaming from the room.

Thankfully, neither came to be.

The figure straightened, and she recognized the small woman.

"Mother!" Godiva sighed and dropped her parasol, her hands shaking. "You scared me half to death. What are you doing hiding in there?"

She wanted to know how much Lady Garland had heard. There was no other way into the dressing closet; evidently, she'd witnessed Godiva's collapse.

And no matter how upset Godiva found herself, never did she seek to sadden her mother.

"Do come out."

Timidly, Lady Garland walked from between her daughter's dresses, so unlike the woman who'd fainted to save Godiva from dancing with Lord Haston, whom she viewed an unsuitable partner.

"I am sorry, my dear," her mother sighed. "I only meant to hang Godiva's portrait and be gone before you returned. Your father said you had a difficult morning. I wanted to lift your spirits."

That her mother thought the oversized painting of her great ancestor in a provocative position would "lift her spirits" was more than a bit depressing.

"Why would Father think I was having a trying morning?"

"Oh, I am not to mention *that*," her mother uttered evasively. "I really should be going. I have been under the weather, as you know." She made to duck past Godiva and escape, but Godiva stepped in her mother's path, blocking her departure.

"Not so fast, Mother," she scolded. Sometimes being the adult in their mother-daughter relationship was downright exhausting. "What exactly did Father tell you not to mention to me?"

"Before I tell you anything..." Lady Garland glanced about the room. "We must—"

And Godiva knew what her mother needed. "Yes, I know, Mother."

Her mother's sense of security was easily stripped from her—confined spaces made Lady Garland feel safe, the same as the color pink did for Godiva—and as a loving daughter, she couldn't bring herself to question her mother's basic need for a sanctuary.

Within a few short minutes, Godiva and her mother had constructed a noteworthy encampment just large enough for the pair of them out of her two sitting chairs, various pillows, and her bedcover. They set a candle close to provide light, but not so close it caught the coverings ablaze.

But her mother wasn't prepared to speak, and Godiva couldn't push her before she was ready.

Godiva thought—not for the first time—that she had given her whole self to life, which was in direct opposition to her mother, who chose to hide. Godiva had known great happiness with her family and close friends but had also experienced great sorrow early in life. Even her friendship with Delilah was much the same. She loved her dear friend, valued their connection, yet Delilah's actions had caused her much grief. But that did not hamper Godiva's ability to be happy for her friend and the match she'd chosen with Canterbourne.

How she'd longed to despise her friend, cast Delilah from her life without a second thought. What would she have gained from that but needlessly hurting another? Losing another? Added to that, Godiva firmly believed the heart wanted what the heart wanted and one had little control over whom the heart fell in love with.

Lady Garland had taken a different path in life, favoring a close relationship with her husband, raising a great child, and keeping all negativity from her circle—as much as she could. She had few close friends and almost never left their townhouse or ventured from their country estate when there.

Godiva had been shocked at her willingness to host the ball the previous evening. True to form, however, her mother had acted faint early on, and Godiva had escorted her to her chambers.

She'd asked her mother, and tried to bribe her father, into disclosing her mother's reasoning behind it all, but both only shared their joint distrust of the harsh world around them. Yet, neither blamed Godiva for choosing to be a part of it.

Beatrice, sitting cross-legged on top of a small pink pillow, looked to Godiva. The sadness in her eyes broke Godiva even more. It was as if she knew her daughter's thoughts and wanted to banish them. Godiva didn't want to be the cause of her mother's pain.

"You cannot protect me from every hurt," Godiva whispered.

"I wish there was no need for any of us to be protected." Her mother appeared small, almost childlike, beside her. "Why are people so cruel?"

Godiva wondered what unpleasantness her mother spoke of. "Maybe they do not see the full ramifications of their actions or the effect they have on others." This was the reason she couldn't stay mad at Delilah and Canterbourne— they were in love, and therefore, oblivious to everything around them. They did not set out to purposefully hurt

Godiva or her family. "What did Father ask you not to mention?"

Her mother fidgeted with the corner of a pillow, avoiding once more. "Oh, he did not forbid me to mention it, only asked I refrain from speaking of it until you had worked it out on your own."

"And what does Father think I need to work out?"

"Your feelings for the Duke of Beargarner, of course."

"My feelings for Beargarner?" Her father had imparted the real reason Marcus had set his sights on her the previous evening. "Why would he think I have any feelings—good or bad—for that scoundrel, Beargarner?"

Beatrice peeked up with a knowing smirk, and Godiva regretted her question. "He saw the two of you leaving your chambers last night during your ball."

Words escaped her—she hadn't thought someone would see her and Marcus depart her room, nor had the thought to look about even crossed her mind.

"Oh, dear," her mother gushed. "He wasn't spying on you."

Godiva laughed. Her father's eavesdropping and spying were the least of her worries.

"He was coming to see me and saw the duke escorting you down the hall."

If her father thought she and the duke had affection for one another, then why would he cast doubt on the man this morning? He could have kept the comment to himself and allowed Godiva to believe Marcus favored her over what her family could offer him. Except that was not how the man worked. It was as if he were more informed on Godiva's situation than she or Marcus was.

"I do not have a *tendre* for the duke, Mother."

"If you say so," Beatrice said, attempting to hide a smile. "I can only speak to what your father shared with me."

"And how is he so sure something between the duke and I exists?"

"He said you had a certain look about you—your eyes were alight."

"How does he know a simple look means anything?" Godiva questioned.

"Because he insists it is the same look I bestowed on him the day we met." Her mother made to stand. "I must be going now. I think you have much to think about."

Godiva didn't stop her mother from crawling from their fort. Nor did she try to stop her from leaving the room.

She was right—as she often was. Godiva had much to ponder.

It didn't matter she looked to Marcus with interest; it mattered only how he looked at her. One could love another —invest the entirety of their being—and still be crushed because that love was not returned.

While Godiva wasn't disillusioned enough to believe she'd loved Danderfur, Plumberly, or Canterbourne, she'd thought there was a chance of love developing and a true fondness for one another to evolve over time.

Had her first instincts about Marcus been wrong, or could he want her—as well as need her?

CHAPTER 12

"*M*ay I help you?" the Garland's butler asked.

"I am here to see Lady Godiva." He repeated the statement for the third time in under twenty-four hours.

"May I announce who is calling?"

He knew the answer would be the same as soon as he gave the man his name. "The Duke of Beargarner." He'd repeated himself to the butler on each occasion, yet the man insisted on acting as if he didn't recognize Marcus nor who he'd arrived to see.

"Please wait here." The door slammed in his face for the third time. No invitation to enter the foyer was issued.

Marcus *needed* to see Godiva—to explain everything, even if she decided to throw him from the house after. And so, he waited, just like before. Hope surfaced when the servant took longer to dismiss him than the previous two times he'd called.

He shuffled his feet and pulled his overcoat tighter to ward off the early evening chill. He'd planned his final visit carefully to ensure Lady Godiva would be at home, and if she once again denied his visit, he would have no other choice but to leave her be, for harassment was not his pursuit. At this time of day, she should be in residence, preparing for their nighttime activities.

The door opened once more, but with a little less force than previously.

"Right this way, Your Grace." The butler issued a curt bow, catching Marcus off guard. "My lady awaits you in the drawing room."

Finally, she was ready to hear what he had to say—or she'd only relented to get him to stop calling. Either way, Marcus would be able to express his apology in person.

His footsteps echoed through the open foyer and the butler preceded him down a long hall. It was familiar, and Marcus knew the ballroom was situated at the far end. Instead of going that far, however, they stopped before a closed door.

"She is expecting you," the butler said before turning on his heels without announcing him.

"Thank you," Marcus called to his retreating back.

Breathing deeply, he knocked on the door.

"Enter," a whimsical voice chimed from within.

Confused, Marcus grasped the knob and turned. Either Godiva had forgiven him or...

"Ah, Your Grace," a woman who most assuredly was not Godiva called from across the room. "Do come in and have a seat."

The small woman—he'd describe her as a pixie if he believed they existed—reclined on a long sofa, a blanket covering her from the waist down and an open book across her lap. She looked much like Godiva, yet older.

"My lady." Marcus bowed before taking a seat in the nearest chair.

"You are quite handsome, indeed," she mumbled as if he couldn't hear her. "My Godiva is a fortunate girl."

Marcus wasn't sure Lady Godiva would agree.

"My lady," he said again in greeting. "I am the Duke of Beargarner, but please call me Marcus."

"Oh, I know exactly who you are." She laughed with merriment at his puzzled expression. "I am Lady Garland, Godiva's mother. I know we look more like sisters, but I can assure you, she is my daughter."

"It is a pleasure to meet you, Lady Garland." He couldn't help letting his gaze wander the room. "Will Lady Godiva be joining us?"

"Heavens, no." She laughed again at some private joke. "She has declared never to speak with you again. Silly child."

"Well, thank you for giving me the news firsthand." Marcus stood. There was nothing more to say. "Let her know I will not pester her further."

"Do sit down." Her words were curt, making it clear challenging her was not wise.

Marcus quickly regained his seat, staring at his clasped hands like a sullen child ready for a tongue-lashing. And he deserved just that—and more.

"Do not look so nervous, Marcus," her voice softened once more. "I did not agree to see you to condemn your person. My husband, Lord Garland, is convinced there is something between you and our Godiva, and I had to see it for myself."

He wanted to ask what she expected to *see*. He was here, while Godiva was not.

"She does not know I agreed to meet with you," Lady Garland confided. "And I do say, she will be rather peeved with me when she returns."

"Returns from where?" Had she departed London? He

would never forgive himself if he'd caused her to flee London to avoid seeing him. "Is there anything—"

"Do calm down. She only went to visit Lady Delilah."

Marcus sat back in his chair, commanding his heartbeat to slow in an effort to focus on Lady Garland.

"Godiva is a strong girl. Your deceit would not cause her to leave her home—you may be handsome and charming, but your powers are not great enough for that."

"I wasn't thinking—" He'd been soundly put in his place.

"Yes, you were." Placing her book on the table before her, Lady Garland tossed her blanket aside and stood, walking over to a portrait hung on the far wall, her fingers lightly caressing the wooden frame. "It is not to say she isn't wounded and hurt, because she is. But she has come to expect such things from men—other than her father, of course."

"Of course, my lady," he mumbled, unsure how to respond to such a direct condemnation of his sex. Marcus didn't know if the woman was lecturing him on being an honorable man in the future or merely explaining Godiva's position. However, he most certainly wanted to hear everything she had to say. It could be his final chance at hope. "I have come to apologize and explain everything."

"And how will she know you speak the truth now?"

He'd believed all along he was speaking the truth to Godiva. Every word, every action—the kiss, for certain—had been genuine. From the moment he saw her in the hallway, he'd forgotten his father's debts.

"I can tell you did not mean to hurt her," she said.

This admission should have alleviated his guilt, but it only led to more questions.

"How do I convince her of my good intentions?" he asked. Short of writing her a letter, professing his sincere apology, Marcus was at a loss as to how to remedy the situation.

They'd met a mere three days ago, but nothing had mattered more to him in his whole life than making things right with her.

"It would be foolish of me to help you, Your Grace," she said, shaking her head as if she were sorry that she couldn't fix everything herself. "Your words and actions must come from your heart, not mine."

"I do not mean to offend, but why are you telling me this?"

"Simple." She regained her seat across from him. "I love my child with my whole heart."

"But I lied to her."

"I am not sure it was meant to be a lie, Marcus." She eyed him, waiting for him to confirm this. "Besides, one can have several reasons for pursuing a certain person. Love and money are not mutually exclusive needs."

Marcus wasn't sure he loved Godiva after their brief time in each other's company, but he was positive that money was not his sole purpose either.

"Given time, do you think she will listen?" Marcus didn't have time, but he'd wait as long as it took for her.

"Do not give her time, Marcus," she instructed. "If you want her, make her see your heart is true."

For the first time in many years, Marcus missed his mother desperately, for she would have given him the same advice. He hoped Godiva would listen to him—and understand—because among other reasons, he would really enjoy having Lady Garland in his life.

"If you must know, she and Lady Delilah plan to attend the Theatre Royal at Covent Gardens this evening." Inclining her head, Lady Garland signaled their visit had come to an end. "And please, do not tell Godiva I sent you her way. I imagine the two of you would have eventually found one another again; I am merely speeding things along."

Marcus nodded. "I will not tell, my lady."

"Very good." She retrieved her discarded book. "Do you think you could love her?"

Marcus hadn't expected this. "I…"

"Oh, you have no need to answer my question." She laughed again. "But it is something you should ponder greatly before making your next move."

He nodded, lacking any response that would endear this woman to him.

"Now be gone before Godiva returns, or Lord Garland catches me meddling in her affairs."

"As you wish," Marcus said with a quick bow. "I do hope to make your acquaintance in the future."

"That rests on your shoulders, my boy."

And it weighed considerably. All of his decisions since arriving in London, his treatment of Godiva, and his inability to realize he could have been honest with her. Much hurt would have been avoided.

The butler was waiting to show him out when he left the room.

Marcus hadn't a moment to spare before this evening. So many ideas rushed through his mind as he alighted Canter-bourne's coach.

One thousand pink flowers—no, blue—she said she thought blue was best.

A short play, acted out on stage to show her his true intentions.

Mayhap a simple declaration from him in front of an audience would suffice?

He discarded the ideas one by one. Flowers could never capture all he wished to say. A scene from the actors at the theatre was too easily misinterpreted. And a declaration? He wasn't confident he knew how he felt yet. How would he ever convince her if she suspected his words did not originate from his true heart?

The ride to Canterbourne's townhouse was short, and he was no closer to figuring out a plan when the coach stopped in the drive. He had limited time to dress and depart if he wanted to arrive before the theatre was filled to capacity.

There was little hope, even with Canterbourne's help, he could locate her in the crowd.

Marcus hadn't had a solid plan for the evening, but he'd never felt surer of his odds at gaining Godiva's forgiveness. If he were anything like his father, he'd be at White's placing several bets. Part of him understood his father's need to risk it all in the hopes of gaining tenfold.

There was no doubt Godiva would improve his life—more than tenfold.

The front door opened wide to admit him entrance into Canterbourne's home. It would be nice to have his own butler and footmen attend him once again.

"Good afternoon, Myers," he greeted the servant whose arms were outstretched to take his coat. "Is Canterbourne about?"

"No, Your Grace," he answered hesitantly. "But you have a caller in the study."

A caller?

Only a limited number of people were aware he was in town, mainly the few who'd recognized him at the Garland Ball. He dreaded coming face to face with Gwen once more after her horrid treatment of Godiva.

The woman, while unpredictable and ever irrational, would not be so bold as to seek him out here.

Marcus wished he'd said something, anything, to defend Godiva before she'd fled. Instead, he'd kept his mouth shut, adding insult to injury by appearing to agree, or at least not challenge, Gwen's affronts.

Before he could question Myers about his visitor, the

servant had disappeared to parts unknown, Marcus's coat in tow.

Entering the study, Marcus did not recognize the fellow standing before the far bookshelf, inspecting the spines of Canterbourne's oldest books. He was dressed in a dark brown suit, but even from where Marcus stood, he saw the elbows were worn, and the cuff of his pants stained from travel. His discarded hat and satchel sat by Canterbourne's desk.

Marcus hadn't made a sound, but he knew when the man sensed his presence in the room for he slid the book back into its spot, adjusted another that was slightly off, and turned toward Marcus.

"The Duke of Beargarner, I presume?" The man's cultured tone indicated he hadn't been sent on behalf of one of Beargarner's estates. "Of course, it is you. You look much like your late father."

Anyone who knew Marcus beyond an acquaintance knew it was in his or her best interest not to mention the previous duke in Marcus's presence. His days in London had afforded him a bit of distance from the situation facing him at home—but it appeared his troubles had, indeed, caught up to him before he was ready.

"What can I do for you, Mr.—"

"Smith, Mr. Smith," the man chimed in.

"Mr. Smith. To what do I owe your visit?" Marcus asked. "I do not believe we are acquainted."

"Ah, yes. You are quite the difficult man to track down." Mr. Smith shuffled back to his satchel, released the clasp, and retrieved a large folder of papers. Marcus was sure they mirrored the many stacks currently residing on his desk at Beargarner Hall. "I am Lord Sothary's solicitor."

"I don't believe I've made the acquaintance of Lord Sothary, either." The name didn't spark any memory with

Marcus, but that meant naught; his father had begged, borrowed, and wagered funds with every gaming hell and loan lord in England proper.

"Lord Sothary has not been fortunate enough to meet you, as of yet." Smith held the papers to Marcus. When he didn't accept the large bundle, the man set them on the edge of Canterbourne's desk. "These will explain everything, but suffice it to say he and your father were well acquainted and partnered on several business ventures—many not as successful."

Not as successful when compared to what, he wanted to ask.

"Well, now that I have completed my responsibilities, I will take my leave." Mr. Smith collected his hat and re-latched his satchel before turning to Marcus, his hand outstretched. "I do apologize for my surprise visit, but as I said, it was quite a task finding you. Good day."

Leery, Marcus shook his proffered hand, then watched the man depart.

Most collectors did not greet him with any type of warmth nor afford him any respect.

They made their demands for payment...informed Marcus of the consequences of non-payment...and eyed anything of value as they departed.

Mr. Smith had done none of that.

What in the bloody hell is going on, Marcus wondered?

The door had barely shut behind Mr. Smith when Marcus snatched the file from the corner of Daniel's immaculate desk. Written in the bold, neat script was his last name, Adair, with his father's first name crossed out and replaced with Marcus. The black lettering had faded with time, his name being the darkest; the edges of the folder were tattered from use. The gathered pages weighed more than the responsibilities hovering over his head for the last couple of years.

His eyes never leaving the papers before him, Marcus took the few steps around the desk and sat heavily in Canterbourne's massive, high-backed chair, setting the folder before him.

Somehow, he knew whatever lay within would change his future, and he only prayed it was for the better because he hadn't anything else to give, nowhere left to go for help. He'd determined when he left Lady Garland that if Godiva would have him for her husband, he'd never ask her for help with his financial woes; he'd deny her dowry, or at least set it aside for their children's use, and would never go to Lord Garland for access to his cargo ships. There were no other means for Marcus to convince her his intentions were pure and came from his heart, not his empty pockets.

With a deep breath, Marcus flipped open the first page, and what greeted him pushed all the air from his lungs, leaving him struggling to pull in another breath but without the sense of how to accomplish it. His mind swam as the words on the page sank in.

He now owned three ships in a fleet of nine, all managed by Lord Sothary's man of business.

All debt incurred from the purchase of said fleet had been satisfied.

Marcus shuffled the pages, finding the sheet signed and dated by *The Governor and Company of the Bank of England*, showing that, indeed, Lord Sothary and his two silent partners, were paid in full on the note taken five years prior.

His father's initial investment of twenty thousand pounds now resided in an account to be used as Marcus saw fit. For a man without a farthing to his name, it was an exorbitant amount of coin, surely enough to pay the salaries of his servants and the crew of three ships until goods could be brought into port and sold.

The minutes passed as Marcus read every document in

the folder, going back several times to make sure he understood everything.

A loud chime echoed down the hall and into the study he sat in, striking six times before going silent once more.

With newfound assurance, Marcus stood as he closed the folder and slipped it under his arm. He had much to accomplish and not enough time to do it in.

The Canterbourne butler met him at the bottom of the stairs. "Your Grace. May I be of service to you?"

"Have a bath drawn." Marcus slapped the servant on the back in good spirit. "And a carriage brought 'round."

"Yes, certainly. As you wish."

"Oh, and rouse Canterbourne." Marcus laughed at the butler's startled expression. It was highly unlikely any servant within Daniel's home would last long if they went about "rousing the lord." "Let him know it was I who sent you. Tell him to prepare for an eventful evening."

CHAPTER 13

*G*odiva took in her new pink dress in the looking glass. It was of the fashion she preferred, high-waisted with a modest neckline to ensure adequate coverage of her bosom. While she was aging, she hadn't yet reached the majority when it was acceptable for her charms to be on display. She'd discarded the sash that accompanied the dress in favor of an ebony one.

She wore her simple brown walking boots to complete her outfit. There was no telling how much walking she and Delilah would do while at the play. Her friend was noted to spend the whole performance moving between acquaintances chatting about town life, recent gatherings, and her upcoming nuptials.

It was no secret Godiva envied her friend's natural way of socializing, speaking with mere acquaintances regarding mundane topics as if she were invested in each one—which, she likely was.

The pink dress, along with a matching ribbon, had appeared on her bed while she'd been out visiting Delilah.

She'd thought she soothed her mother's concerns about

Marcus and any attachment her parents believed she and the duke shared. But with the dress came the knowledge they were still worried about her. Or more to the point, they sensed someone had hurt her.

Glancing at the clock on her mantle, she snatched her drawstring purse from her bed and headed downstairs to await Lady Delilah and her parents. She looked forward to the distraction of attending the outdoor theatre; there was more than enough activity to keep her mind from wandering to Marcus. It had taken all of her efforts to pay attention to Delilah and her aimless ramblings about Lord Canterbourne's townhouse décor, which she insisted she must change once she became his marchioness.

If Delilah noticed Godiva's preoccupation, she'd been polite enough not to mention it.

A knock sounded at the door as Godiva reached the foyer.

"Please, let them know I will be right out."

The butler nodded before turning to the door.

Godiva moved quickly down the hall to the drawing room her mother favored. She'd begged Lady Garland to accompany them this evening, but her mother still insisted she was under the weather, and a night in the frigid London air would cause her more harm than good.

The door stood open, and she spied her mother curled up on her favorite lounge with a book in hand. She'd been told as a child that the ultimate escape could normally be found within the pages of a book—and Godiva agreed most times.

Beatrice appeared so at peace Godiva was hesitant to disturb her instead marveling at the youthfulness of her face.

But she never left the house without saying goodbye to one or both of her parents—and at the moment, her mother was the lesser of two evils. She was unlikely to bring up the subject of the duke and his many calls over the last days.

"Mother."

Startled, Beatrice looked up from her book, a smile lighting her face. "Oh, my dear, sweet child." Her gaze traveled from Godiva's face to her feet and back again. "Lovely. The black sash is a marvelous touch, but don't let your father see. He will think his years of showering you with pink were not to your liking."

Godiva agreed to remove the black sash before returning home this evening in case Lord Garland waited up for her.

With a quick kiss to her mother's head and a warning to get some rest, Godiva departed.

The carriage ride was uneventful, and traffic was light for the time of day. Delilah's parents kept to themselves and allowed the girls to chat.

Godiva took in her friend's refined attire. Ever since Delilah's betrothal, she'd taken to wearing form-fitting dresses that cascaded to the floor about her feet. No more high-waisted, pastel gowns for her. And her décolletage inched lower and lower by the day.

It was as if Delilah had gone from being Godiva's childhood friend to a grand lady of the *ton* overnight, leaving behind her childish interests in favor of refined living.

Godiva hoped one day it would be her going from high-waisted pastels to boldly colored, flowing silk…but it wouldn't be today or even this season. Or likely ever since Godiva's large frame would be unsuited for such a dress.

"Godiva, my dear?" Delilah's mother, Lady Davendore, asked. "Is your mother well? I have not seen her about lately."

"Oh, yes, she has been spending much of her time reading."

"Ah, I greeted her the other evening in the receiving line, but after that"—Lady Davendore snapped her finger before continuing—"she disappeared into thin air. I hadn't had the chance to commend her on the success of the evening or invite her for tea."

Godiva was always tentative to discuss her mother's less than sociable nature with others, however Lady Davendore and her mother had been friends for longer than Godiva had been alive—and more to the point, Delilah's mother knew Beatrice wouldn't accept the invite.

Lady Davendore would certainly be impressed to know Godiva had organized the evening herself, though she'd allowed her mother to believe she'd had a hand in things.

"I will give her your best regards, my lady."

"Oh, take in the crowd," Delilah cried with glee, her face pressed awkwardly against the windowpane. "I do believe I've spotted Lord Canterbourne...over there, waiting for my arrival. He is ever the gentleman."

Godiva sincerely hoped Lord Canterbourne was not lingering outside the theatre waiting for Lady Delilah's coach, for it would not be a leap in imagination to expect Marcus would also be not far from his friend's side.

Godiva had agreed to the evening out with her bosom friend—not her bosom friend, her ex-betrothed, and a duke who'd openly lied to her.

Thankfully, Lady Davendore saved her. "Now, Delilah, you cannot spend every waking moment *with* Lord Canterbourne, *thinking* about Lord Canterbourne, or *chasing* after Lord Canterbourne. It is simply not done and may cause him to distance himself from you."

Godiva trusted, for her friend's sake, Canterbourne wouldn't do that.

"But Mother," she wailed. "We are in love and are to be wed."

Both Lord and Lady Davendore shook their heads in unison as if they'd long ago given up harnessing their daughter's overactive sensibilities.

"Drat! That was not him anyhow." Delilah leaned back from the window and crossed her arms about her chest, wrinkling the fine silk. "I do hope this line is not a lengthy wait. We will never make it to our box before the play begins." Which meant, her friend did not like missing out on time spent preening in front of the madrones of high society, seeking favor with the future Marchioness of Canterbourne.

"Never fear, girl," Lord Davendore spoke for the first time. "The queue will go fast. The evening is long, and the crowds aplenty."

Which meant she had a large number of people to annoy that wouldn't be him.

As promised, the line of carriages moved swiftly. Before long, they were walking amongst hundreds of people. They trailed several paces behind Delilah's parents as they moved through the crowd, only stopping briefly to congratulate Miss Everden, a friend of Godiva's, on her recent betrothal.

"I do believe you will make a wonderful bride," Godiva confessed, eyeing Delilah at her side, who clearly waited for Everden to address her betrothal. "You both will have beautiful nuptials and families to follow."

"Oh, I do believe that is true," Everden said before excusing herself when her mother signaled their need to find their seats. "Do excuse me. It was lovely to see you, Godiva—and you as well, Delilah," she added almost as an afterthought.

Next, they encountered Mr. and Mrs. Jakeston, along with Ellington, Mrs. Jakeston's young sister. The couple looked uneasy and wary, as they'd only recently wed and were finding it difficult to acclimate to London society, or so she'd heard from some dowager duchess or other while having tea with Delilah and Lady Davendore a few weeks prior.

"Mrs. Jakeston, very nice to see you again." Godiva took

the woman's hands within her own. "And Ellington, you are lovely this eve. You know my dear friend, Delilah." She released the woman's hands and grabbed Delilah's arms, pulling her forward.

Her friend mumbled a greeting, but her attention was focused elsewhere, scanning the crowd.

"How many times must I insist you call me Ruby?" Mrs. Jakeston insisted. "I wasn't aware the theatre drew such a large crowd." She turned to her sister and continued. "Ellington, you do remember Lady Godiva?"

Unfortunately, the fiery redhead next to her was also distracted, her tall frame allowing her to look above many heads and avoid participation in the conversation.

Godiva pledged to herself she would not be envious of every woman's height. There was no point in cursing her short, rounded stature.

"I cannot thank you and your dear, sweet mother enough for working so diligently sewing all those quilts for the children's beds," Mrs. Jakeston gushed. She and her friend, Lady Haversham, ran an orphanage for injured children. Godiva and her mother had visited several times, and they both enjoyed making the children special gifts.

"It is our sincere joy, Ruby." Godiva smiled. It was the one place her mother never argued about visiting. "We are preparing another special delivery—this time, scarves!"

"Oh, how lovely! Is that not wonderful, Ellie?"

Again, the tall young woman ignored her sister.

Godiva stared between the sisters—the disconnect filling the space, the silence louder than the commotion of a thousand people, deafening even though they stood within a horde of folks. In her unease, Godiva felt the black sash around her waist, complementing the pink of her dress perfectly. And she thought of giving Ruby something pink to let her know her own family issues would work themselves out. Ellington would eventually see her older sister for the person she was—a caring, loving sibling.

Godiva's fingers continued to rub the black material about her waist. She'd initially felt shameful when her mother had pointed out the disregard of her father's gift, given with the thought of love.

But now, Godiva knew she didn't need his reassurance any longer.

Lord Garland had sought to assure his only daughter that, though the duke had lied and misled her, all would work out for the best because he and Lady Garland would always be there for her. But a time would come when Godiva needed to refuse their favors and heal on her own, even if only to prove to herself that it was possible.

The silence had stretched out awkwardly between the parties, partly because Delilah and Ellington were focused on searching the crowd, and partly because Ruby stared at her as if she knew Godiva was working through something on her own.

"Mrs. Jakeston?" Godiva tentatively asked.

The woman smiled at her question but didn't speak.

"Do you think the girls at Lady Haversham's orphanage are fond of pink?" The moment the words left her lips, Godiva knew it was what she wanted—and what her parents had hoped for, at least one day. "I have many dolls, trinkets, shawls...all in the loveliest shade of pink."

"And you have no use for them?" Ruby's eyebrows rose in question.

"No, I have long outgrown them, but only recently realized they would be better suited to another, someone who would truly appreciate their beauty." There was no going back on her gift—and Godiva had no wish to change her mind. The many trinkets and tokens had been given from a place of love and caring, and she wanted to do the same for another. Gone were the days when a pretty hair ribbon or fancy doll would mask the hurtful words or actions of others.

Godiva longed to be strong enough to meet others head-on, hear their words, see their actions, and learn to accept them without support. A day would present itself when Lord and Lady Garland would not be there to protect her anymore.

"We would be happy to accept your donation," Ruby nodded her thanks. "That is, when you are ready."

"Yes, I will instruct my housekeeper to have the lot of it packed and prepared within a few days."

"That is overly generous of you, Lady Godiva." Ruby released her husband's arm and clapped with delight. "I do believe Lady Haversham and the children will be overjoyed at the timing of your gift."

"The time is now." It was exactly what Godiva needed. She'd move past the betrayals of the Duke of Beargarner on her own. "And, Mr. Jakeston, my father says your shipping endeavor is becoming fruitful in the best of ways." It was the height of impropriety to mention business dealings, but what was one to discuss when topics such as weather and fashion did not suit her any longer?

"Lady Godiva." He issued a small bow before continuing, "I fair very well, thank you. Please give your father my best and thank him for his support."

"I surely will." Her father had assisted Harold Jakeston and his brother when they'd partnered in a venture to ferry cargo to and from France. It had been a successful arrangement for many months. "It was lovely to see you again."

Moving on, Delilah and Godiva only nodded to known acquaintances until they reached the Davendore box just as the performers took the stage. The play was a tragedy, much as was the tendency, and this did not disappoint. Godiva laughed throughout the first act at the outrageous stunts of the characters, but she noticed a drastic turn toward the severe when the curtain lowered at intermission.

"Come with me, Godiva," Delilah pleaded. She was surprised her friend was able to keep still for so long. "Please, let us acquire a drink before intermission ends. Say it is okay, Mother?"

Her imploring look, which had been on Godiva, now turned to her mother.

"Of course, but," she paused to wag her finger at her daughter, "you must return before intermission is over—and for heaven's sake, do not hang all over Lord Canterbourne."

"Did you see him?" she yelped. "Is he here?"

"Lord have mercy on that man's soul," her mother whispered. "Do go, my dear."

They only made it a few yards before Godiva heard her name called.

Turning to greet whomever it was, she wished she would have kept her head down, played like she hadn't heard her name, and hid the remainder of the evening.

As it turned out, she now faced the duke in all his well-tailored glory. The man simply didn't understand she did not want to see or talk to him today—or any day.

Unfortunately, her manners were better than his and dictated that she play nice and maintain the poise befitting her position as a lady. They would surely have tongues wagging if she confronted him here.

Instead, she gave him a slight curtsy and an indifferent, "Your Grace." Her insides felt anything but indifferent.

The man looked downright jovial. His smile showed perfect teeth.

She hadn't the foggiest idea what he was smiling about.

"Lady Godiva." He offered his arm, which she didn't take. "Walk with me."

"Oh, I most certainly cannot abandon my dear friend," she protested, reaching for Delilah but only finding air and open space—Delilah was suspiciously missing from her side. With a quick turn of her head, she spotted her horrible friend a few feet away with Canterbourne. Could the night get any worse?

"Lady Delilah appears in no need of a chaperone at the moment," he whispered knowingly as if they had a secret, just the two of them.

Which they most certainly did not.

"My Lord Canterbourne!" A voice called to Godiva's left, and she cringed. Visibly cringed. "Dandy great coincidence seeing you and Lady Delilah here. And Beargarner!"

As was his habit since their scandal, Lord Plumberly failed to acknowledge her or so much as glance her way. It was childish and hurtful. If it didn't completely lack in decorum, she'd kick him in the shin. She still hadn't any notion why he'd added his name to her dance card at her ball. Thankfully, she hadn't had the need ever to find out.

No one greeted him in return, which delighted Godiva. She smirked internally, lest Marcus think the smile was meant for him. Delilah and Canterbourne were focused on each other, and Marcus still stared at her, his grin never dimming.

"Ah, so where are you chaps headed after the play ends?" Plumberly raised his brow in question, but again, neither of the men answered—his question hung in the air. "I was thinking about going to White's myself. You have a membership, right Canterbourne? Maybe a few hands at the card table?"

The scene before her was laughable, for the only person looking at Plumberly was the one person he would not make eye contact with.

"My, my!" a stuffy voice called. "Tell me it isn't so...

Plumberly and Portly reunited and back in love?" Lady Gwendolyn flounced—that was the only way Godiva could describe her movement—as she stepped between Godiva and Marcus, her evening gown twirling about her legs before settling.

Mentally, Godiva counted her one good deed—in return for her lovely dress—was not smacking the woman.

"I knew I recognized the fondness returning the other evening."

Godiva at once noticed Lady Gwendolyn's dangerously low neckline, with a large ruby perched solidly between her pushed-up breasts. She wondered if the woman did not have a mother or father or aging aunt to dissuade her from leaving her home in such a wanton dress.

This night was turning into anything but the anonymous evening she'd planned. The night and conversations were supposed to revolve around Delilah and her future, not Godiva's past.

She scanned the milling crowd, expecting to spot Danderfur lurking in the shadows, as he was the only missing piece to the tragic comedy that was her unfortunate life thus far. It would have been wise to call off sick, as her mother had.

For a moment, she pondered this might be why her mother avoided *ton* gatherings outside the controlled environment of her own home.

"I shall alert the paper immediately." Lady Gwendolyn clapped with merriment. "The pair of you will have delightfully fat babies!" She laughed at her own comment—the cackle of a witch if Godiva were to voice her opinion. Which she didn't because that would only invite the woman to spout more hateful comments.

Though no one would have listened if Godiva did hurl an insult back.

"Come, Marcus," Lady Gwendolyn said, making a grab for his arm. "You may escort me to my seat."

"I will not be escorting you anywhere, not tonight or any day hence." Lady Gwendolyn recoiled in shock and Beargarner's sharp retort. "I will depart with the lady I choose, and that, Lady Gwen, is not—nor will it ever be—you."

Delilah and Canterbourne took their eyes off each other and settled their startled gazes on Marcus.

"And you, Lord Plumberly." Marcus turned a stealthy look to the gentleman Godiva had once thought to spend her remaining days with. "You are a blockhead."

Marcus stepped toward the man, and for a moment, Godiva thought she would grab his arm to bring him back, let him know the man meant nothing to her, and his horrid treatment of her was so far in the past it was as if it had never happened.

However, she held herself back from reaching for his arm.

"You passed on the opportunity for a future beyond all you deserve—all any man present deserves—and not a piece of me resents you for that." Marcus poked his finger into the man's chest as he spoke each word. "For now, I have the occasion to convince Lady Godiva I am indeed the only man for her."

Godiva stared at everyone but the Duke of Beargarner.

CHAPTER 14

The crowd around Marcus went silent, staring at him in awe.

Except for Godiva.

She stared between Lady Gwen, Delilah, Canterbourne, and Plumberly.

He wanted to ask Plumberly why he continued to stand before him, stock-still with astonishment.

The old Marcus would have challenged him to a duel; show the coward he could not treat a lady with such vagrant disregard and get away with it. It was inconceivable a duel would change Godiva's feelings about him. The centuries of proving one's mettle by brute force were long over. A lady sought words more than actions.

Yet, that would not advance himself in Godiva's eyes. Marcus knew that much about her. His time and energy would be far better spent gaining Godiva's forgiveness.

All he needed to focus on was Godiva—and gaining her pardon and hoping she blessed him with the compassion she bestowed on all those around her.

Something he was worthy of now.

He only prayed he could put into words everything he longed to say, the many realizations that had come since their short acquaintance started.

"Lady Godiva." Marcus offered his arm to her, starting over. "May I escort you to your box?" He had no idea who she'd arrived with or where her chaperone was, for it would be highly improper for Lady Godiva and Lady Delilah to attend alone. Godiva was nothing if not a woman who followed societal norms when she must.

She still refused to look at him, which he deserved…and it gave him time to take in the sight of her. Truly look at all the goodness that was Lady Godiva. The occasion to do so before had been limited.

Her fashion sense was on the demure side, which he favored as opposed to the almost scandalous dress that was common, and favored by most, in recent years. Her gown, gathered about the waist, accentuated her curves in the most pleasing of ways.

Her brown hair, not too dark but definitely not blonde, was piled on top of her head, exposing her supple neck. When she was his duchess, he'd adorn her throat in the finest gems he could buy. He would have teardrop earrings crafted to match, and maybe a bracelet as well.

He watched Godiva's chin lift as Gwen, recovered from his words, stared daggers, her rage ready to boil over. Marcus had been on the receiving end of Gwen's sharp tongue more than once, and it was not a place he wished Godiva to be, especially with such a crowd gathering. But his Godiva would face the opposition head-on, as she'd done many times before in her life.

He wanted to tell her she wasn't alone, and if he had his way, she'd never be alone again.

He willed her to look at him. To really see the man he believed himself to be. To realize he was deserving of her.

But again, why would she think his intentions anything more than selfish?

Much had changed in the last several hours—he was still wrapping his mind around everything—and he only desired time to speak with her.

He no longer needed anything from her—and still, he desired her. The least likely person he'd ever known had solved his financial problems.

His late father, the previous Duke of Beargarner, had made one smart decision in his life.

And that had been to sponsor Lord Sothary's venture to the Americas.

As far as Marcus had been able to assess, his father had taken the last of their money and given it to Sothary, a newly appointed baron, and had then forgotten about the whole affair. Maybe he was too used to failing at everything to keep a record at that point—or maybe he'd perished before noting the investment in his journal.

Hell, the possibility existed he was too drunk even to remember handing over the money.

Marcus didn't know.

One thing was for certain: Lord Sothary had honored his side of the venture, seeking out Marcus even though he knew of the previous duke's passing a few years before. And now, Marcus was free to court Godiva without any doubt of his intent, and all the time in the world to convince her of his honorable purpose. But telling her proved difficult if she wouldn't give him a moment of her time. He'd underestimated her anger toward him.

In the back of his mind, he replayed Lady Garland's words, "Do not give her time," and "You can want a person, but also equally need something from them." Or maybe he remembered the conversation that best fit the outcome he desired.

Either way, he was here, as was she.

He only needed to rid himself of Plumberly, Gwen, Daniel, and Delilah. To his dismay, no one budged as most of the gathered crowd stared at him. Gwen stared at Godiva. And Godiva had become preoccupied with a pleat in her dress.

The crowd around them thinned as people returned to their boxes, or the general seating area, to watch the second act of the performance.

Shortly, the six of them would remain with only passing vendors to notice.

For the first time, Godiva raised her gaze to his. The pain in her expression, the desperation of her stance, and her resignation were evident. He could not let her crumble.

She was everything he'd never known he needed: confident, compassionate, and accepting of her own abilities. Aware of who she was and what she had to offer another. Which was why she was so upset with him.

Marcus was willing to accept everything—to love and cherish her for whom she was, not what her dowry professed she was worth. In his heart, he'd never have taken Godiva to be his wife based on the interest in her father's cargo ships. He kept his arm outstretched, willing her to take it—to tell him there was a chance, maybe not today, but one day. A hint that she'd listen and forgive him.

It was much like their first evening together.

He'd avowed she'd make him the happiest man in all of London if she just took his arm—but now, the tables had turned. His happiness would only come from hers.

If she took his arm, he'd do everything in his power to make her the happiest woman in all of England proper.

"Please, let us go..." Marcus whispered. And to his immense shock, she stepped toward him and set her hand on his arm. That was all the initiative he needed to pull her close. "Before I do something likely to cause yet another scandal."

Marcus didn't say another word as he walked away with Godiva on his arm, straight from the theatre. He called for the Canterbourne carriage. He wouldn't ask her to sit through the remainder of the play, for she appeared to be only partly keeping things together. If she were upset by his forthright decision, he would bring her back another night to see the performance. At that moment, he wanted her away from the cruelness of Gwen and the indifference of Plumberly.

NEITHER SPOKE AS THEY WAITED.

Godiva stared straight ahead. He wondered what went through her mind. She had every right to be angry with him, hurt by Gwen, insulted by Plumberly, and disbelieving of Lady Delilah.

If Marcus hadn't been there, not a single person would have come to her rescue.

Again.

Maybe Delilah was accustomed to Godiva taking care of herself, permitting others to speak to her in such a horrid manner, but that was done. It was past time Godiva cared for herself and stopping allowing such harm to befall her only to make those around her happy.

Thankfully, she hadn't fled.

Marcus would have been hard-pressed to decide to follow her or stay to defend her.

A footman offered her assistance into the carriage, but Godiva didn't release Marcus's arm. Stepping forward with her, Marcus handed her into the waiting vehicle before entering behind her.

Upset as she was with him, she longed for him to be close

in this moment—and he'd stay with her as long as she desired.

She chose the forward-facing seat and sat directly in the middle. Reluctantly, Marcus took her unspoken cue and sat across from her on the emerald velvet cushion. His position brought into focus the extreme odds of her dress color to the emerald velvet of the seat. It was much as he viewed their lives. While she'd spent years pursuing the favor of society, he'd chosen a reclusive lifestyle. She had grown up in a loving home with parents who did their best to make her feel cherished and appreciated. And in contrast, after his mother passed, Marcus had spent years on the coattails of a father who cared so little for his son and their family legacy that he'd spent every farthing they'd possessed.

His breath hitched when he took in her face. The sorrow her eyes held, the defeated slump of her shoulders, and the way her fingers worried a seam in her dress. He felt a physical pain inside from her dejected attitude. He wanted back the confident demeanor he'd witnessed at the ball when she'd challenged him to demand what he wanted and not take no for an answer. He longed for the woman he'd spent a few private moments within her bedroom. While she'd been irked at Gwen's cruel words, she'd still been daring, able to see the situation for what it was.

Gwen had projected her own insecurities onto Godiva because she was threatened by the beauty Godiva presented —and she must have instantly known he'd, under no circumstances, be hers again. It was puzzling that Gwen imagined, after everything she'd done, the grief she caused, he'd see fit to resume their relationship or begin any semblance of friendship.

Especially after meeting Godiva, Gwen and what she represented did not appeal to him.

A woman who played games and toyed with his emotions

on a daily basis could not make him happy. Happiness he believed possible when he looked at Godiva.

Godiva appeared wounded and tiny across from him. He wanted nothing more than to pull her to him, embrace her, and whisper all of the wonderful things he knew to be true about her. All the positive things no other had taken the time to discover about her.

And he sensed there was more still to her he hadn't been allowed to learn as of yet.

Years would not be enough.

Decades, maybe.

What Marcus knew for certain was that he wanted the time with her, desired her above all else.

He needed to make her believe.

Rapping his knuckle on the side of the carriage, he yelled out the open window to the coachman. "The Pool with haste, Mitton," Marcus called, confident the man needed no further explanation. Next, he turned to Godiva. "Do hold on, Godiva."

Before he could say anything else, the coach slowed and turned around, heading back in the direction they'd come from. There was an easy way to prove he cared—that his intentions were not based on what he needed, but all about what he wanted. Now and forever.

Godiva's arm swung out, and she held herself upright as the coach straightened out and headed toward the Port of London.

Her father might deem it inappropriate for females to visit the port or know about business ventures, but he wanted things to be different between him and Godiva.

"Where are we going?" She looked up from under lowered lashes as if waiting to assess his answer. "Lord and Lady Davendore will worry."

"We will make one stop, and then I will bring you home, I

promise. We will not take long." Marcus hoped after she saw what he'd seen earlier in the afternoon, she'd reconsider listening to him. Then they could return to her family's home to talk, or he would leave her safely at home if that were what she demanded. "I must show you something first."

"Whatever is so important that needs attending this late in the evening?" Leaning toward the window, she peered out, her brow furrowing. "Are we headed toward the port?"

"I assure you this is very important." He reached across the open space between them to take her hand, stopping her from toying with the seam of her dress. "I promise."

The roads this late in the evening were dark and deserted, many hardworking men having already traveled home for the evening, leaving only the occasional unsavory type milling about the streets.

The carriage traveled from the well-cobbled roads of fashionable London to the ruddy, pockmarked, hard-packed dirt of the streets closer to the port district. The avenues widened to accommodate the transport of goods to and from the docked ships.

"We aren't far now."

Her hand remained in his grasp, for she hadn't made any move to pull away, though she did keep her eyes trained out the window. He hoped this would assuage her mistrust of him, allowing her to see him with open eyes as she had when they'd first met. If only she would give him the opportunity.

CHAPTER 15

*N*o one had ever stood up for Godiva before. Never had anyone said people's behavior to her was not right or correct or kind. Her parents had taken the stance of showering her with gifts after the incidents, for they were rarely present when Godiva was hurt or insulted. Others preferred to act as if it didn't happen, or they hadn't heard, much as Delilah had done at the theatre.

She couldn't bring herself to speak, but she'd relented and taken Marcus's arm. Trusting him to care for her.

She wasn't ready to commit to anything more than what this moment held for them.

But Godiva would listen.

She owed him that much for doing what no one else had.

He'd discovered what lay below the surface, looked beyond what everyone else saw—an aging, portly woman who'd failed at marriage three times. Marriage? No, she hadn't even made it that far. Her dowry and her father's title had attracted several suitors, yet none had bothered to know her.

And now she sat in a darkened carriage, traveling through

a seedy part of London toward a destination she could only guess at, with a man she'd longed to trust and believe in—yet, in the end, had deceived her like the rest.

She looked down at his hand, clasped with hers. A sense of security filled her. She remembered the same feeling taking hold the night they'd met—an overwhelming sensation that this man would do nothing to hurt her.

"Never in all my years have I ever felt this safe with another," she whispered. It was all she had, bringing together all the feelings she felt for him, about him, and with him. Not once had she hesitated to enter his carriage, nor allow him entrance into her private chambers. "I still feel protected."

She didn't know what the words meant to either of them, but they were the truest words she'd ever spoken to another.

"I will guard you always."

"Then why did you not tell me you sought business ties with my father?"

He sighed, but kept a firm hold of her hand, his fingers gently caressing her palm through her glove. "I hadn't had the time." He was not fool enough to play ignorant of what she spoke of. "I was more interested in knowing about you than sharing about myself. Besides, if you had known upfront, would you have danced with me? Kissed me as you did?"

"I do not know," she replied. "You took that decision from me."

"And for that, I am truly sorry. However," he paused as if pondering his next words, "I am not, nor will I ever be, sorry for that night. *Because* I thought I needed something from you, it allowed me the opportunity to meet you—a woman whose outlook on life has changed my own."

"How so?" She would keep asking questions as long as he was willing to answer them because after all she'd been through, Godiva needed to understand why he would do the same to her…lie to her as so many had. Was she not worth the truth? She'd never been given a chance to ask the rest of them, but with Marcus, it was different. She hadn't cared about the others enough to seek answers, demand explanations. She needed to know why from Marcus—but from there, she couldn't fathom what was next.

Would they never see one another again, like Danderfur?

Would they move around society, ignoring one another, like Plumberly?

Or, would she have to see him every day, experience his happiness with another, like Canterbourne?

She knew now that she would not be able to bear seeing Marcus with another, yet the thought of a life completely devoid of him was unthinkable and far worse.

"Why me?" It was the thing that weighed heaviest on her.

"'Why *not* you' would be a far more astute question."

"Do not jest with me, Marcus." She sighed. "Why me as opposed to Lady Gwendolyn? I hear she is very wealthy in her own right, and she is beautiful. If not her, why not another woman like her?"

She held her breath, waiting for his response. It could change everything, or it could impact nothing—or both, all at the same time.

"Can I tell you a story?" he asked.

"I do not want a story…I want the truth." The desperation in her tone was unmistakable.

"You are right," he said, although Godiva hadn't any idea what she was right about. "Years ago, I courted Lady Gwen. As you've pointed out, she is exactly what society tells me I should select in a wife."

Godiva had known there was something between the pair —but years ago? "She seems much attached to you still."

"I cannot speak for her feelings or perceived attachments."

She didn't want him to be the same as all the rest. She silently willed him to continue, prayed her worst fears would not be recognized.

"Godiva, she abandoned me." His voice pleaded with her to understand, but he was nowhere close to telling her everything. "When I learned of my dire financial position—the horrid mess my father had left me—everything in my world changed. I was no longer the heir to one of England's wealthiest dukedoms. Not even remotely."

Her heart ached for him. Not because she forgave him, but for the simple fact that she'd been where he was; she'd experienced betrayal that deep and cruel.

"In that time, my estates and the people who lived there and depended on me became my top priority, not courting Lady Gwen. I could no longer—with a good conscience—give her expensive gifts of jewelry or fancy gowns. No, I sold many things from my home just to keep my people fed and warm during the cold months."

"I did not know." She'd thought the worst of him without giving him a chance to explain. "You sought me out for the sake of others?" It seemed far less heartless of him to sacrifice his own future to improve that of those he cared about.

"At first, yes."

"And then…what changed?"

"Meeting you."

Godiva pulled her hand from his, her anger flaring once more. "Meeting me? How can our meeting change anything? You are still in need of my dowry—"

"Godiva, please listen," he pleaded, reaching for her hand again. When she hid it in the folds of her skirt, he let his palm rest on her thigh. The mere touch sent bolts of lightning coursing through her. "I never wanted your dowry."

"Oh, excuse me if I find that hard to believe."

"I am not a man to take from another. I know how it feels

—I could never do what my father did." He sighed, allowing his hand to fall when she shifted away from him. "I only needed a bit of cargo area on one of Lord Garland's ships to alter my current situation—and with that, my fortune and future would have changed."

"But by then, you would already be attached to me—for life." Godiva shook her head. She'd been unsure if learning of Marcus's purpose had been a blessing or a curse, and she was still confused. "Then what did you plan to do with me? Leave me at one of your estates to while away the remainder of my life?"

"My one flaw—I hadn't thought that far into the future." Had he truly expected to find a simpering, pitiful creature who'd willingly run into the arms of any man who took any bit of notice? Had he been under the misguided impression they'd be doing one another a favor by accepting the match?

Godiva nearly laughed at the ridiculousness of it all.

"Just far enough to see your fortune returned?"

"Not my fortune, but a newer, brighter future for every Beargarner descendant and servant."

"And now?" she asked. "You said things have changed. Is that why we are here?" She waved her hand toward the carriage window.

When she settled her hand on her lap again, it gave him the opportunity to grasp it once more. He leaned in close with his next words. "Why we are here is important, but everything changed for me long before this." He nodded to the window.

He was confusing her more by the moment, and she couldn't help wondering if that had been his plan.

"The moment I met you, I knew I had to have you, everything else be damned." He was a hair's breadth from her, and if she leaned just a bit forward, their lips would meet. But then he'd stop talking, and Godiva desperately needed to hear every word. "You are magnificent, charming, beautiful, witty, an amazing dancer...must I go on?"

She wanted him to go on. To never stop telling her all she longed to hear.

So, she'd continue to hear him talk. To do that, she leaned back in the velvet seat, ready to listen, and far enough away from his lips that the urge to kiss him receded—slightly.

"And why did you not tell me any of this before?" she asked.

"I tried, Lord, how I tried, but you wouldn't see me."

She'd denied his calls several times, secretly hoping he wouldn't give up, would keep pursuing her. What had she hoped to gain from that? If he had continued to show up at her doorstep several times a day, for weeks on end, would she have believed his intentions were pure?

"You did not trust me enough to ask for my help—without your scheme—to gain my father's consent?"

He sighed, leaning back against his seat. "I wish I had, but, unfortunately, women such as Lady Gwen came before you. How was I to know you were any different than the women I'd met before?"

Unwisely, Godiva had judged him in line with the men who'd come before him, as well.

"You could have given me a chance." Godiva crossed her arms, thinking how unfair she was being. She'd taken his actions at their worst because of her past experience with men, yet, she expected him not to do the same. "Where does this leave us and our relationship now?"

CHAPTER 16

*I*nstead of answering, Marcus looked out the window again, his disbelief and awe as fresh as it had been mere hours before. "We are almost there. May I show you?"

The carriage slowed as they turned from the main street onto a smaller drive that led toward the water. As the carriage creaked along, Marcus took joy in the shouts and merriment of the few workers who remained late. A couple yelled, with a few shouting their reply. They were not angry calls or anxious shouts but singing and much laughter.

Across from him, Godiva turned to her window once more. He knew exactly what she saw, and the wonder that filled her expression mirrored his from a few hours earlier. Men entering and exiting ships, their arms laden with crates, bags, and trunks.

"What is all this?" she asked in wonder. "I've always been told the dangers of the ports, drunken men and less than savory women, dangers of falling cargo and coiled ropes. But this—this appears straight from a fairytale."

She stared into the distance, spotting one ship larger than

the others, lit brighter than the stage at Covent Gardens. The gangplank, dock, and sides of the ship were illuminated by hundreds of lanterns.

"We are here," he proclaimed. They'd stopped before the ship she'd been admiring.

"The Beargarner Express," she read aloud from the ship's side.

Marcus marveled at the sprawling white letters, taking it all in once again. The name was ironic, for with its size, he suspected it was not built for speed. "Do you remember how you asked if someone had ever given me something...something so special it would be a betrayal ever not to keep it?"

"Yes." She'd meant the many gifts given to her by her father—his guilt-inspired gifts. "But..."

"At that time, I hadn't any notion of what you spoke," he confided. "People had only ever taken from me, returning nothing. Will you come outside with me?"

The carriage door opened, and Marcus leapt out. For a moment, he feared she wouldn't follow, but then she took his outstretched hand, and he smiled, his body filled with hope.

"My lady." He waited for her to step down.

Which Godiva did, his thrill contagious—and surprising him, she smiled in return.

"We will return in a few moments, Mitton," Marcus addressed the coachman, who nodded in answer.

"I will await you here," he answered, looking about as two men rushed by him. "Can Anderson accompany you down the dock?"

"Thank you, but no." At the coachman's leery look, Marcus continued, "I am familiar with the captain." He'd met the man not long ago, but knew the skipper ran a tight ship and that he and Godiva were safe on his dock.

"Right, Your Grace."

Arm in arm, he and Godiva preceded toward the ship.

"It has your name."

"It does." They came to a stop before the vessel where it gently rocked in the water, both of them admiring the large craft.

"Why is that?" Taking her eyes off the grand ship before her, she focused on him. "And why bring me here?"

When he'd given the coachmen the directions, he hadn't fully understood why he decided on The Pool either or what he'd gain from it, but he needed to prove to her he had other options—he didn't need Lord Garland's ships or her dowry. His financial windfall had come from the most unlikely of places.

Most importantly, with his fortune returned—or at least solidly on the way to recovery—he didn't *need* her, but he still wanted her. His feelings for Godiva hadn't changed.

"It is all mine. Well, a large majority of it, as there is one other investor."

"I am happy for you," she said skeptically. "I truly am, but again, why bring me here?"

"Because there is no one I'd rather share this with."

Her eyes snapped to his, and she stared so intently Marcus feared she'd see through to his very soul. "What does that mean?"

"It means, regardless of whether I am penniless and without resources, or wealthy beyond my wildest dreams, I will desire you. Only you," Marcus paused, finding it hard to go on without collecting himself as his emotions threatened to overcome him. He hadn't a single person to confide in or count on since he'd lost both his parents the day his mother died. "Nothing—none of this"—he waved his arm at the ship docked a few paces from them—"matters if I do not have you by my side to share it with."

He couldn't stop talking, telling her anything and every-thing—all of it true—to keep her here. "I cannot say what overtook me that moment in the hall when you about knocked me over, but I am forever changed and incomplete without you. You showed me the simple pleasures in life with those brief moments in your chambers. And then, with Gwen and Plumberly, you were justified in your anger and hurt, but you did not allow their deplorable words and actions to ruin you."

She looked away. "If I had done that, I would be like my mother and never leave our home."

"I've let many things in my past—my mother's death, my father's withdrawal—ruin me, ruin my perception of the world, but not you." He rubbed his palms together to still his need to reach for her. Many men had stopped their work and stared at them. "I crave you in my life. With you, I know I will not allow the harsh realities of this world to crush me." He paused. "Godiva, please say something..."

She held his fate in her hands, and Marcus trusted her not to crush it.

And that was when she did the one thing that broke his heart quicker than anything else imaginable.

Godiva turned and walked away.

And with her, she took everything he'd begun to imagine his future held. Love, passion, contentment, family, and a home. Nowhere would be home without her.

CHAPTER 17

*G*odiva ran toward the waiting carriage, her skirts held high in her hands—but the space took a lifetime to cross. He'd said all she'd needed to hear, longed to hear…every word had been perfect.

And she'd started doubting every decision she'd made since they met.

There were limited things she knew for certain. One, every man, with the exception of her father, lied. Two, her instinct was not to be trusted.

Yes, Marcus had been less than truthful with her, but she'd never once given him the chance to tell her a lie because she'd expected he would be deceptive if asked anything concerning his past.

Her instinct was telling her to forget all that came before and start fresh—for herself and for Marcus.

But Godiva didn't know where or how to begin.

The thought of dispelling every hurt, every cruel word, every treachery imposed by others seemed more than daunting. It seemed like a task too great to undertake on her own.

But one that would have to be done for her to move forward and achieve any measure of happiness.

Was she strong enough to put all her faith in Marcus and forget the many lies foisted on her in the past?

Could she or her parents survive another scandal if she chose the wrong path?

These were things she wasn't strong enough to face on her own.

The tears came uncontrollably, blurring her vision. She couldn't see the carriage any longer, but she kept moving, knowing it must be in this direction.

"Godiva," Marcus's frightened voice called. "Stop, please."

The carriage should not be this dreadfully far; they'd only walked a few moments.

"You are crying!"

Yes, the hot tears flowed down her face, and Godiva hadn't the urge to stop them. Maybe if she mourned long enough, it would all be as if it never were. Every cruel word said to her, every deception played upon her, every pink gift given to her.

Gone.

As if it never were.

Every wrong done to her erased.

If she just ran far enough, hid well enough, sheltered herself from it all…

Finally, she stopped, her sight so impaired by her tears and her racing heat she couldn't tell what direction she ran and what, if anything, lay in front of her.

Arms, strong and secure, instantly wrapped around her, pulling her close—Marcus's sandalwood scent invaded her every sense, bringing with it the calm she felt whenever she was near him.

"Godiva, my dearest," Marcus cooed. "My love. Hush, please. I am sorry. Anything I can do to make things right, I will. I will leave now, never bother you again, but please do not cry." He said all the wrong words now. "I will take you home. Everything will be fine."

Now, she didn't know if she cried because he'd finally told her all the things that she'd wanted to hear or mourned the thought of a life without him.

He couldn't go. In no way did she want to be deprived of him.

"Then why did you continue with your ruse?"

His answer held the possibility of breaking her heart all over again.

"I could not—would not—appear less of a man before you," he confided in a whisper. "I never intended for you to know how far my title and estate had fallen into disrepair. It was my responsibility to fix all within my power...or be resigned to debtors' prison."

"You would rather live in the harsh confines of Newgate than admit you wanted me solely for my inheritance?"

"That was the farthest thought from my mind after we met." His arms tightened once more about her. "I fear I cannot put into words the way you make me feel—but it is as if nothing else matters but knowing you are here and that you'll always be by my side. I prayed the day would never come when I would have to tell you why I'd originally set my sights on you, but I now know what a mistake that was."

"I would have heard your plight, and together we could have found a way." She wanted to hold him for as long as she could—clutch him tight and never let go. But too soon, his arms loosened, and he stepped back—or did he push her from him?

It didn't matter because his eyes were on her. Deep, brown, honey-colored depths, trained on her. Only *seeing* her.

Instinctively, Godiva tilted her chin slightly up, and his lips were on hers, possessively.

And she realized, her resistance to him had been futile.

Their fate was destined to be the moment they'd met, and her instinct about him was surely right.

She wanted him—and everything that came with it.

Godiva sank into him, his mouth drawing all the hurt, pain, and anguish from her and leaving nothing but the promise of better things to come.

A future of happiness.

It was her turn to push him away, as much as she dreaded the act. Her hands moved between them, pushing at his chest, giving her space to say what needed to be said.

"Marcus, I cannot know how it happened, or even when, but I love you." It was the simplest thing to say, not a single catch. "I love you now, and somehow, I even loved you before."

Sometimes there were no words to express what you felt —it was actions that spoke volumes.

And at that moment, nothing screamed, "I love you" louder than Marcus's actions.

One moment, she was on the dock, professing her love... and the next, she was in his arms, their mouths locked once more, sealing their fate.

EPILOGUE

*M*arcus, her dear, sweet, attentive husband of a mere few weeks, pushed the door to his —*their*—London townhouse wide and stood back, allowing her entrance.

"Should you not carry me over the threshold?" Godiva teased.

"I've carried you over every threshold from here to my country estate and back. Remember the inn in Bath?" He set aside the large, awkward package he'd guarded their entire journey. "Why would today be any different?"

With little effort, Marcus swept her into his arms and stepped across the threshold—and into the place that they'd decided to call home, at least until after Delilah and Canterbourne were wed next season. The Beargarner family townhouse—a three story building that'd been left neglected for nearly two decades.

Setting her down, Marcus nodded to the package tied securely with thick brown paper and twine. "Can we please open it now? The suspense is killing me."

Godiva eyed the gift given to them on their wedding

morning by her parents—well, mostly her mother. She wanted to wait to open it until they'd settled into life, traveled to his country estate, and returned to town. By then—which was now—Godiva hoped she'd have inserted herself into his life so genuinely he couldn't imagine living without her.

Then she would untie the twine and reveal her final secret.

"Are you sure you do not wish to eat before we start unpacking and settling in?"

"We ate with your parents only moments ago," he said. "Now, we open that. Do you not want to see what your parents gifted us for our wedding day?"

Godiva had spent years trying to unsee the image hidden within the wrapping, and she would save his eyes for as long as possible. "Maybe tomorrow."

"No." Marcus grabbed the cumbersome package and carried it to a small table. With all the delicacy she knew he could muster, he set it down flat, then pulled the twine free. "I cannot wait. Even more intriguing is your reluctance. So, now it is, my love."

Godiva's cheeks heated, imagining his expression when the twine came free and the paper was folded back. "Really, Marcus, this can wait." She grabbed for his hand as he pulled the paper back, a note falling to the floor at their feet.

He snatched the card from the ground. "It is addressed to you, Duchess of Beargarner. I rather like the sound of that."

There was no denying she approved of her new title as well. She took the envelope; her mother's swirling print covered the parchment and her wax seal fastened the note.

With uneasy fingers, Godiva broke the imprint and unfolded the letter within.

. . .

My dearest Godiva,

I know this letter finds you—and your new husband—at a time of great joy. This package holds all I've ever wanted for you in life. You were not named for Lady Godiva because you were a plump, most demanding baby—although that explanation worked for a time—but because I had hoped you'd be like her. She lived her life without regret or fear of consequences, which enabled her to be happy. In a time when women were only objects and the station of their husbands dictated everything, Lady Godiva fell in love with a man unworthy of her, of her purity and goodness. And while I cannot confirm many details from her time, she knew a love beyond all that her station should have allowed. That love was for her people, despite the hardships she faced when she challenged her husband.

You may wonder why this horrid portrait—yes, even I know it is horrid—means so much to me. It is simply because Godiva had the confidence and fortitude to commission it. It didn't matter that it depicted her most mortifying moment. She threw caution to the wind and did everything needed to save her people.

There is much I longed to do with my life. Unfortunately, we both know I have not experienced any of it...but you, my child—

Godiva glanced heavenward to stall the tears that blurred her vision.

"Godiva, is all as it should be?" Marcus asked with alarm.

Nodding, she went back to reading.

...but you, my child, have never let the betrayals and scandals, dampen your excitement for life. I envy that greatly.

In short, my Godiva, your lord has come for you—do not let him go. Together there is nothing the pair of you cannot attain; a long, happy life is guaranteed.

With my fondest love
~Mother

GODIVA RAISED her gaze to the man beside her—his hair longer than was proper, his shoulders broad from the labors on his estate, his eyes keen with knowledge, and his arms outstretched, calling her to him.

Yes, he was everything she'd ever desired in a husband she'd never thought herself worthy of.

And there would never be a day she would let him go.

"I love you," he whispered. Leaning down to take her lips, he paused. "And I will never let you go, either."

She hadn't spoken aloud, yet he knew her thoughts.

Marriage—and a life with a lord of her own—would be a glorious thing.

And the painting could most certainly wait until tomorrow.

ALSO BY CHRISTINA MCKNIGHT

Don't miss the *USA TODAY* Bestselling Series
A Lady Forsaken Series
Shunned No More, Book One
Forgotten No More, Book Two
Scorned Ever More, Book Three
Christmas Ever More, Book Four
Hidden No More, Book Five
A Lady Forsaken Box Set (Books 1-5)

Craven House Series
The Thief Steals Her Earl
The Mistress Enchants Her Marquis
The Madame Catches Her Duke
The Gambler Wagers Her Baron

The Undaunted Debutantes Series
The Disappearance of Lady Edith
The Misfortune of Lady Lucianna
The Misadventures of Lady Ophelia
The Season of Lady Chastity

The Desires of Lady Prudence

Lady Archer's Creed Series
Theodora by Christina McKnight
Georgina by Amanda Mariel
Adeline by Christina McKnight
Josephine by Amanda Mariel

Standalone Stories
For The Love Of A Widow
Bedded Under the Christmastide Moon
Bound By the Christmastide Moon
The Lady Loves A Scandal
Earl of St. Seville: Wicked Regency Romance
Fated For The Duke
Fortunes of Fate: Prequel Story
Fortune's Final Folly

Connected By A Kiss Series
A Kiss At Christmastide (Book One)
By Christina McKnight
How To Kiss A Rogue (Book Two)
By Amanda Mariel
A Wallflower's Christmas Kiss (Book Three)
By Dawn Brower

ABOUT CHRISTINA MCKNIGHT

USA TODAY Bestselling Author Christina McKnight writes emotional and intricate Regency Romance with rebellious women and maverick heroes.

Her books combine romance and mystery, exploring themes of redemption and forgiveness. When not writing she enjoys trying new coffeehouses, visiting wine bars, traveling the world, and watching television.

www.christinamcknight.com
christina@christinamcknight.com

AUTHOR'S NOTES

Thank you for reading *A Lord of Her Own.*

If you enjoyed *A Lord of Her Own* or any of my other books, be sure to write a brief review at your favorite retailer.

I'd love to hear from you!
You can contact me at:
Christina@christinamcknight.com

Or write to me at:
P O Box 1017
Patterson, CA 95363

www.ChristinaMcKnight.com
Check out my website for giveaways, book reviews, and information on my other projects,
or connect with me through social media at:

Twitter: @CMcKnightWriter
Facebook: www.facebook.com/christinamcknightwriter
Goodreads: www.goodreads.com/ChristinaMcKnight

Sign up for my newsletter here: http://hyperurl.co/CMNL

I'd love to thank all those who never gave up on me! Especially Marc McGuire, Erica Monroe, Lauren Stewart, Angie with TwinsieTalk Book Reviews, and Debbie Haston and Theresa Baer (my super awesome group leaders). You have all been very patient and wonderfully supportive of my eccentric ways.

A very special thank you to my editors, Erica Monroe (Quillfire Author Services) and Chelle Olson (Literally Addicted to Detail).

Cover art credit to Sweet 'N Spicy Designs.